Cover image courtesy of Salisbury Cathedral
and photographer Russell Sach
Cover design and book layout by Simon Crummay
Typset in Garamond and Cormorant Unicase
First Published by Amazon 2023

ISBN: 9798871361405

Magna Carta

Conversations in Salisbury 1260

A novel by
Sue Allenby

Contents

Foreword

In 1260 in Salisbury, the January cold and the dismal February rains linger on into early spring. Then, when the watery sun finally appears in April for more than just a day or two, from time to time people notice a stranger walking through Salisbury's marketplace. There's nothing odd about that, except that this one has been seen wearing very smart red leather shoes and carrying his embroidered gloves. In the mud and dust and detritus that everyone has to pick their way across, that immediately sets him apart. The gossips wonder who he is.

Salisbury market is where news happens as well as where it is passed on. This stranger is already causing some consternation in the ironmonger's shop, as he has begun to call regularly on alternate Wednesdays to collect a package that a courier delivers. The quick-witted girl behind the counter is putting two and two together. Cecily Clerk is from one of the families who do much to help the friars feed and clothe the poor each winter, now the weather seems to be deteriorating year on year. Their own news-gathering network is generally quite good, but this is usually local as real news of importance doesn't travel well. When it does arrive, at least around here, Salisbury market is the place to be.

Neither Cecily nor any of her family or friends can have any idea about what will transpire, of course. Just one year, 1260. It hasn't been very eventful here so far, although there are plenty of travelling days left before the year's end.

But there is a little more you need to know from the beginning, as well as about this fine new city of Salisbury, itself barely forty years old.

✝

It's the little things, isn't it? I had no ulterior motive at all one weekend, just looking through some old papers, when I remembered that once I had been idly musing on something missing from the great body of work that Archbishop Stephen Langton had left us. Why couldn't I find it–this famous 'inspired' address he had given in 1225, after he had consecrated the Trinity Chapel, the first part of Salisbury's new cathedral church to be built?

In fact, I must have been still thinking about it as I went to sleep that night, because when I woke up–I knew, I just knew…

It happened to be Trinity Sunday, and by the end of the day I was sitting at my computer, staring at the blank screen.

This novel is the result.

✝

A heartfelt 'thank you' to everyone who has listened patiently, and espccially to Simon and all my family for their help and their fortitude.

Eight hundred years on, we here know how strong the pull of Magna Carta can be. These thoughts and writings–and inevitably all those sleepless nights as I lived in the 13th century for a while, again–along with profits from this book, I am giving to Salisbury Cathedral.

SUE ALLENBY
Salisbury, December 2023

The Dawn

There is a moment at daybreak, just one moment when the air is no colour you could describe. It is not quite the softest gold or rose-pink or ash-tree bark or even what you may imagine the colour of light to be, because it is still forming itself into the early dawn and you are privileged just to be there to see it. The utter stillness and the silence is broken by birdsong, and by hedgerow rustlings and tiny claws skittering over leaves. On this autumn day, as yet it is our robin and the blackbirds I can hear. In the dawning, a fox barks. He is a shadow against a growing space of sunlight, but I know where his den is, and how he weaves along his hunting trail through the trees edging our garden.

Salisbury is waking up and tumbling out of bed. Young Nobby the carter will be in his stables already, tending to his horses and turning the hay. Our dairyman will milk his cow and take the pail, covered with a cloth, to each of his customers so they can fill their jugs. Fires are being resurrected, as some children burrow deeper into their beds. Soon the bell for Prime will ring out clear across the valley.

I lie here, between my wonderful linen sheets. Thank you, Ellie Gardener, for telling me never to buy new linen if I can find the finest quality old linen on the second-hand stall in our marketplace; it is indeed much softer and better. And thank you again for darning the holes so beautifully for me. What it is to have found a group of friends this summer. Such friends have been missing from my foolish life for so long. Rob, Ellie's husband, will be busying himself with the fire and planning his gardening day in The Close because the daylight hours are lessening. Eustace Clerk, padding down to the outhouse, while Meg will be resurrecting their fire and stirring the porridge. And now I can hear a thud up the track, for here comes Bernie, his boots munching the gravel, as he arrives to help my Ned out of bed. I must be one of the most fortunate of men. I had never thought I would be writing anything about my life, but when it was mentioned to my new friends that I was considering it, they wished to be included because of all the surprising places we had discovered where our lives had touched before we ever met. This century spans my lifetime, which is longer than that of this new city. I can give you just a glimpse of this lovely place, more at peace with itself and its neighbours than with the wider world, a world of which it knows little, but suspects much. That is how it is in England. We think it is probably a troublesome world out yonder, if only we knew what was going on, which of course we don't. We learn most of what we do know randomly, from rumours in the marketplace.

News that isn't local, reaches us slowly or not at all. The canons in the cathedral church will know more, but even they may not know all that I am going to tell you.

Gradually, over this seemingly uneventful year of 1260, two winters after our new and glorious cathedral church was consecrated, we are finding out that someone whom many here thought they knew so well, who gave himself to this city for a third of his lifetime had, even before New Salisbury was begun, been at the centre of a storm that could change the world. We don't know if that will be so because we cannot see into the future, but I can understand the possibilities.

I make no apologies for using its Latin as well as its English name. Most people don't seem to know anything much about this Great Charter, as it is called, but it just may turn everything upside down. Someone called Simon de Montfort thinks it will, apparently. But the little we know of him is what we heard from a silk merchant. My friends are sure this charter isn't all of the answer yet, this fragile thing, but you have the sense that some day it just could just lead to that answer.

They say that after three fits and starts, from 1215 over just ten years, in 1225 finally everyone endorsed the fourth new issue: the king and the pope and the barons of England, who perhaps all now see it as their own safeguard against chaos, a written framework for the workings of the law. The king needed a grant of money for his French wars, and they had all agreed, this time without any coercion.

And because of this charter, it is not the king but the law that is now paramount here in England, make no mistake about that. Even if there are times when some are tempted to evade its irksome terms. And when it doesn't always seem to work so well, hold fast to this principle, for we have surely been through worse before, and probably will again. But the ground has shifted. And there are questions this charter forces us to ask. They expose our world with its darkness and its longings, as well as colouring it with light and hope.

For this is Magna Carta.

It's the little things, isn't it, that lead to the big questions, and it does throw up some very big questions: What is justice? What is freedom? What is our common law? All this we learn from chance meetings, and the right probing, from memories recalled, and such surprising discoveries, and above all, from the young, with their insatiable curiosity.

Part One
THE APPRENTICE

I am going to begin this story of my life by taking the easy way out, saying that I have often been in the wrong place at the wrong time. But if I am going to tell you all of this, then you should know these things: Epiphany came late for me.

Sometimes, I suppose it just happens that way. Firstly, the accident of birth, then the roads you take, the foolish decisions you make, the dreams you chase until reality catches up with you and you don't even know who you are any more.

I hope I do now, but back then it was a different story. I have completed two full apprenticeships for two different trades in two different places, all because my pride would not allow me to admit pursuing the first was a mistake, and I wanted to "save face." Somehow, it is harder if you are quite good at something, because that goes with the awful feeling you are letting someone down. And then guilt keeps you from ever owning up. All those years, not wasted exactly, but foolish. I see that now.

I have lived in Salisbury twice, but only Bernie, my colleague, business partner and above all my greatest friend–until recently my most steadfast one-and-only friend–was the single other person who knew that. New Salisbury is just forty years old, so that's not bad going for someone who doesn't even come from here, is it? Why did I come in the first place, and why did I come back with my tail between my legs? Perhaps it wasn't all like that; I tell myself now it was because I preferred being the observer that no one remembers,

17

but I'll tell you this story as we go along.

✝

This is the accident of birth that brought me here: the seventh child born of the owner of a flat-bottomed boat who scraped a living catching eels in the Fens. The two children who came after me were puny. The girl, nearly two years younger than me, was born small and weak. She was found one day, dead at the field's edge, face down in a puddle. She had always looked after little Joseph, because no one else seemed to have the time.

How I hated that life. I have a lot of faults, but I hope I don't whine. As ever, I accepted today, closed my mind to it and resolved to do a good job of weaving those darned eel traps till kingdom come if necessary, while for tomorrow, I hatched all kinds of childish escape plans, like hiding in dykes or just running off into the unknown.

Then a miracle happened. I have no idea if God had heard my fervent prayers, or those of my little brother for that matter, who went to the church more often than I did, sometimes just to talk to our sister Emma, who seemed to live on for him. I knew he didn't like eel-fishing either, but he was a quiet kid three years younger than me, and we didn't have much in common.

I must have been about fifteen I suppose, when a stonemason from the great abbey church at Ely watched me and him one day, and saw how well we worked, weaving those eel traps. He came back a day later and offered father two small gold coins to take us away to train us as stonemasons. I know now that is the opposite of what should happen: such apprenticeships are coveted and costly. No wonder father let us go without any hesitation at all and mother just told us to behave ourselves. I remember my brother held us up for a bit while he walked slowly behind me, stopping at Emma's grave before he went into the church to say a final goodbye.

It wasn't far to Ely from the damp place where we lived, near the osier beds that grew there. We youngsters slept top to tail because there were so many of us, so now someone would have a bit more room.

We went off with this man; me elated, Joseph in a daze, and for about a year we learned about cutting and carving stone before he told us we were moving on to New Salisbury. They had finished the Galilee porch for the old abbey church in Ely and nothing much exciting was happening there at the time. He had been hired as the master mason for a very big project. Their Galilee porch for business deals and where women could go was quite famous, I think, so it is not surprising Master Nicholas would be in demand. He would call himself Nicholas of Ely now he had been recognised as a master mason for working on such a well-known piece.

I had never heard of Salisbury, new or old. I knew I was quite good at what I did, so I had plenty of confidence. Joseph didn't have any. I think he still missed Emma. She was eight when she died, and had taught him everything he had then known, he said. I protected him from the rough and tumble sometimes, but heck, he was three years younger than me, so I had to have my own life too.

Salisbury was a complete shock. I don't know what I thought I was coming to, but surely not to just a boggy field and a mad bishop. I decided to keep quiet. To have to start to build a new cathedral church from scratch, oh please not! Keep your head down, smile and shut up. My brother spent his life looking dazed, but the priest in charge of the construction work (yes, it really was that mad a place) kept an eye on him, so he relieved me of that responsibility, at least.

†

The eager market traders would probably tell you a different story. They couldn't wait to leave behind the little hill fort city of Old Sarum and the soldiers in its castle. Under the benign eye of the bishop, and so long as it was within his overall plan, what they did was up to them. There was sunshine all around and sunshine in their heads, so their building site, which also took in his new market square, was a merry place.

You would have thought it would have been the same for the cathedral canons, wouldn't you? Some of them were a good deal harder to budge. Like me, all they could see was a boggy field and they dreamed up all sorts of excuses for dragging their heels, even though they had each been allocated a large plot of land in what would become The Close.

"Perhaps it is quite comfortable up here after all, just for the moment, you know. He's put Canon Elias in charge of all the building work, so let's see what sort of fist he makes of his own house before we must do ours." Word in the boggy field was that Bishop Richard was getting annoyed.

Canon Elias of Dereham, whom very soon we all called the Master, had arrived here in 1220, a year or two after us. It was whispered he was a top lawyer, unusually completely trusted by everyone; so a discreet and an honest man. He had been in exile until recently, but had then returned to build that famous shrine in Canterbury for S. Thomas Becket in marble, with gold and jewels. So, no ordinary canon then. But once here he started work immediately. My goodness he did! Stonemasons were allowed to volunteer to help him for a set period to build his new house, and similarly us apprentices, to fetch and carry and learn. Once or twice, I noticed Joseph deep in conversation with him, that unlikely priest in charge, and I realised that I, for all my confidence, could never have discussed anything with the canon other than my work. I wondered in fact if they were talking about Emma. Joseph and I had never known each other well as children, but, looking back, I think it was moments like those where our paths started to diverge. The new house looked more interesting and immediate to me, so I applied to move over to the plot he had chosen. Joseph didn't have the confidence, so he stayed in the trenches with the foundations for the cathedral church.

Leaden Hall, The Master said he would call it, because it was going to have a lead roof. No expense spared, then. It fair took my breath away. He knew exactly what he wanted, and I mean exactly. No leeway there for adjusting as you went along, as I was aware masons often did.

Once his site was drained into the river, we worked with such precision under his quiet guidance, you would have thought he had been doing it all his life. We would be using Divine geometry in the construction of the new cathedral church obviously, but for a house? Master Nicholas would use his own knowledge of geometry, but this man knew what it all meant as well, in terms of relating every aspect of the construction to God. No leeway there either then! He impressed me, and it was fascinating, watching his house being built. It saved me from the trenches over the way, for a while at least.

When we weren't working on or preparing the site and creating the Yard for the new cathedral church, there wasn't a great deal for us stonemasons to do in our own time in those early years, before enough of the new city was established. The carpenters had built us a lodge, which was like any male hideout, I would guess; smelly, slopping with ale and a bit coarse. We devised games to play in the hall, like bowling balls from one end to the other, around the central hearth without setting the wooden ball you had bowled on fire, or you would lose your points and that's another mug of ale you owe someone. Otherwise, we could walk up the hill to Old Sarum. When we got there, we were never quite sure why we had come. So much for the 'high life.'

Old Sarum, the waterless city on the hill fort two miles away was clinging on, but it was becoming a sadder and a harsher place. You could see that some new tenants had taken advantage of the empty plots and were talking the place up, after they had tried to talk the rents down. It was not immediately obvious what would happen to it all when the cathedral church with its clergy had finally pulled out. "Could take forever," both the optimists and the pessimists chimed together.

"I know that some of the trades have gone, with more likely to follow, but isn't that an opportunity?" said the optimists.

"What do you mean we don't have a forge any longer? So, who shoes our horses then? What about the taverns closing? Not enough trade? Surely not! Mistress Honeybee is still here. She'll be selling the honey down there soon if the taverns aren't taking it for mead," said the pessimists.

According to the locals, the soldiers were sourer than ever, and even if we went in little groups we became an easy target. You wouldn't want to go up there on your own. The schools run by the Church were open and the tied peasants were still farming the land. You had to feel sorry for them as anything that had made their miserable lives worth living would steadily fall apart. The choirboys and lay vicars still lived in the place and would continue to do so until the canons' new houses were built and staffed. The bishop had a point. Even the hard-to-shift canons will surely grumble their way down the hill soon. Bishop Richard would be looking for new blood if they weren't careful.

There are things you don't consider at the time, but for the boys and any others who did not have the means to ride down there, all that walking they had to do back and forth must have worn them out. We had a temporary church in which to worship on site, but the old cathedral church up on the hill was used still and surely would continue to be until enough of the new one had been built to get at least a bit of it consecrated. Better get on with it then; go and join little brother in the trench.

From the start, as soon as news of the project spread, stonemasons had swarmed here from all over Europe and even from North Africa to work on the cathedral church. "New!", they must have said, "Let's get in there, right at the beginning!" They couldn't wait. Real stonemasons, you see. They have lines of communication so rapid that our government could learn a thing or two from them.

English masons came here from all over this country too, not quite as diverse of course, but not uniform by any means in language or custom. Even within the system of government imposed on us by the Normans, some local traditions or common law from the old Anglo-Saxon kingdoms endured– "customs" they were called–and especially, I suspect, those from the Danelaw where I came from, as did Canon Elias, of course. Sometimes there were more freedoms there. "Different?", I have heard the Fenlanders say, "Us? No, it's everyone else who is out of step." For me, travelling from the Fens to Wiltshire and later, to Exeter, was an education.

I am sure William the Norman did his best to beat us all down, but towns seemed to grow up, almost but not quite, outside his system where, unless you are a free man, or even if you are semi-free, you still have obligations to the people above you, and there you are, stuck scraping a living, as well as bowing and scraping to those who are higher up. Farming is so important, of course, but it is all based on this system, so it is a very hard life.

If I am worried about something and can't get off to sleep, one certain remedy is trying to work out if farming could be made more productive so there is enough food to go around, and how the people who produce the food could share in the wealth that is created in the towns, so they could afford to buy the things we make here; and how food produced in one part of the country could be taken to another part on the roads we have, without upsetting the whole system that prevents all this from happening in the first place... You know nothing more until daybreak.

It is rather complicated to explain, but it certainly felt a lot more 'Saxon' down here in Wiltshire than over there in Ely. You can almost shake hands with King Alfred's memory in this part of the world. Bishop Richard held our land in Salisbury, but he was modern in that he needed money and lots of it for his building works, so he was looking ahead rather than backwards just at who was obliged to whom and for what. A good and caring man, and people appreciated him, I can see that now.

Without the stonemasons' network, news doesn't spread fast. Had you been in church I expect you would have been told that King John had died unexpectedly, in the autumn of 1216. Joseph and I came to Salisbury following our year in Ely. By the end of those years before we started building upwards in 1220, we heard that the uproar over the old king's tyrannical behaviour had subsided, with the barons having laid down their arms and the French prince who had come here to depose him, gone home.

We supposed the king's council would rule England until the new boy king came of age. Given the misery and war and extortionate taxation everyone had endured during King John's reign, even at the time it seemed to us it all had to be for the better. A new city could thrive in peacetime.

News from 'outside' was scarce anyway, but right here, of course, everyone was much more excited about having a new city;

you could almost touch the thrill of expectation on both of the building sites.

We heard that our bishop was attracting the church reformers here, the scholars, in their droves it was said, with their new ideas on education for the lay folk and private penance and him bringing his own ideas on how to care for his flock. I couldn't see what it was all about and how these church reformers could help anyone. Everyone said that the canons wanted to teach us at least some of what they know. Actually, everyone just wanted to learn how to make a good living.

It was on the water meadows where he was planning to build the cathedral church. Daft, I thought. At least Ely, in the Fens where my home was, had been built on higher ground, and on oak piles. I just shook my head. Drainage at all levels became the order of the day.

We had heard that many new towns were under construction around that time, but I can see now that Salisbury had the smell of success about it right from the beginning. Their much-loved bishop, Richard Poore, (the madman I had met who walked excitedly up and down the foundations of the cathedral church all the time) was famous, so I understand, but he needed revenues to help fund the immense cost of his building works, so he would make sure the city would thrive, prosper, and grow. The Archbishop of Canterbury was helping all he could, selling Indulgences to people who could afford them, something that would give them time off in purgatory against all the sins they had committed, so he too would support the Fund.

No one had expected the time and money lavished on the new cathedral church to be repeated for the hopeful, cheerful, industrious people who came here to the new city, but even without it, they set to work with a will. Everyone agrees it has all been a great success and that it continues to prosper even though it is still rumoured that all may not be well in the world outside. There are always rumours because real news is hard to come by, but we never know if they are true or not.

"Thus it was when New Sarum - New Salisbury - was born", the chroniclers will write. People here laugh and in their confident local voices, disagree. Listen to them chattering: "No", they say, "isn't it joining up the little Sarisburie settlements in this valley, so we must be Old Sarisburie, not New Sarisburie. We always were known as Old Sarisburie." They don't hear the 'l' outsiders use; you see. The bishop calls the hill "Old Sarum", with its Latin ending. Well, he would, wouldn't he? No one appears to mind much either way.

Even before the building work itself started, someone said that the new laws that King John had torn up had been reissued twice already, with more land to be released for farming and grazing; "Whether it was suitable or not", the sceptics muttered. No one I knew had been told about a Great Charter that contained these new laws, whatever they were. If the weather is good, the harvests are good and fewer people die of hunger, but then there are more mouths to feed. It is simple really. I think this was the extent of most people's understanding in those days.

It sounded so ungrateful, but I had decided already that this life wasn't for me. Enduring hard work was in my nature I suppose, so no point in sulking, just do it and learn. To have any credibility looking for another trade, I decided I needed to finish my apprenticeship. Only a few more years to go. Keep your head down and smile. Was I even thinking straight? Why did I need to become a stonemason if what I intended to do even then, was afterwards to become an apprentice to some other trade somewhere else? Saving face and pride really was what it was about, not wanting to look ungrateful and protecting my image; I had yet to learn about humility. The time came to begin building upwards: we were starting on the eastern chapels first.

†

Just after I finished my apprenticeship, and had a lot of jugs of ale poured over my head to prove it, my brother fell off the scaffolding. The poor little beggar hadn't been concentrating, I suppose. He didn't deserve that, and I easily made up for the work he should have done. Fortunately he hadn't been too high up, or hurt himself as badly as we had all feared, as it turned out. It took a while, but when he was well enough to walk around again, we saw his left foot was a bit twisted and he had a slight limp. I stayed around for a full year after it happened, not only to earn enough money to have some to take with me when I left, but also to make sure my brother was alright, because if I ever made it back to Ely, mother would want to know. It became clear he wouldn't ever climb scaffolding again, but by then The Master, whose housekeeper had tended and fussed over Joseph as he slowly recovered, was teaching him to read. He limped around then with a big smile on his face, so I could see that it all suited him much better. None of us could say we weren't looked after here. You never know, do you? If I hadn't stayed there to finish as an apprentice stonemason, I would never have known about Joseph's accident.

I had realised however, during those years, that it was Salisbury itself that was beginning to enmesh me, so I could never really leave. What a mess I was going to make of my life. I suspect I knew even then that one day I would be back. How much easier it is to understand yourself in old age and wonder how, or even if, you should have done things differently.

At the time I just let myself succumb to some of the enthusiasm radiating out of the city. This place was going to hum, but I had, of course, realised too late that weaving withies didn't translate into stone for me, but probably into woodworking. And I didn't want to build a cathedral church, but something my small mind could cope with; perhaps boats or houses or furniture. Wrong place, wrong time. I just couldn't admit I had been wrong, or worse, that the master mason had been wrong to bring me here, so it was much easier eventually just to say I was moving on to Exeter, which wasn't too far away, but a safe enough distance so that no one would try to find me. Move on is what masons do, it happens all the time. Some of the masons here thought there wasn't much activity at the time at that particular cathedral church and were at a loss to understand why I wanted to go there, but that was not what I was concerned about. Someone may take me on as an apprentice carpenter or joiner I hoped, although of course I never said I was going to have to start again at my age.

Before I went, something made me walk through the new city here, listening to the happy people still coming down from Old

Sarum. Listening to their voices:

"Farewell Old Sarum, you windy old hillfort."

"Farewell soldiers in the castle (we never liked you anyway)."

"Farewell to Mistress Honeybee or whatever-your-name-is, your bees make such good honey. Why not come to sell it in our new marketplace?"

"Farewell to not having enough water or enough space. Welcome to where we are, to the land of the five rivers running in the lovely valley below, where the sun always shines."

Years of my life wasted, I thought, but I put on a brave face. I had to say thank you to Master Nicholas for all my training, and to wish him and the team well. I knew how shocked he had been at first when he discovered that it would be Canon Elias who would be designing the new cathedral church rather than him, but I think he could see eventually that they had very different skills. They both understood geometry, but I knew from watching his house being built, that for Canon Elias, the Master as I still call him, every ratio, every angle, every measurement, every space had a meaning related to theology and to the beliefs he and the clergy shared, that was deeply significant to them, and was why he gave no quarter on adjustments. It wasn't an easy discipline for the masons, but it is why this church would be so beautiful, beyond the human eye, of course. I had learned something here, after all.

I could no longer detect any frustration or animosity on Master Nicholas' part. In fact, the recent period when my brother was ill with some sort of fever, seemed to help to bring them together. The Master, together with his master mason, did lead a wonderful team.

Joseph would no longer be a mason either, of course. Isn't it strange, the way things turn out? The day I left, I ran back and gave him a hug and told him I had decided where I should go, because it would suit me better. "Goodbye, Reggie", he said. "I'll be alright now."

 "Goodbye, Joseph,"

Two brothers who had barely known one another.

†

I think before we go any further with the story in Salisbury, I had better tell you about what happened when I left Salisbury for Exeter, or at some point you may learn of things that I should have helped explain, from the two families in Salisbury who have become my friends. You may be surprised at how here and there our lives almost touched, at how near and how far Exeter can be.

I shall say right here that I found Exeter to be a good place. It is remote, and very old–a Roman town, I believe. I like the fact it is at a distance and goes at its own pace. When I went there, I was still wondering about building boats, but I dismissed it in favour of other woodworking, as boat-building is a skill perhaps more difficult to transfer elsewhere. Let me be honest, back to Salisbury.

I had all my savings from the year after my apprenticeship as a stonemason had finished. It wasn't a great deal, but it had to be enough, together with my determination and the little samples of stone I had carved secreted in my satchel, to buy me an apprenticeship with some hard-pressed carpenter or joiner. I would promise to work all hours of course, and he could profit from all I did. It didn't matter much to me where I lived. If that sounds hard, then for five years it truly was.

It had not occurred to me in Salisbury that Exeter and indeed Devon itself would be so different. Devon is not a timber-framing county as I would now understand it. In Exeter there were buildings with decorative, good close timber frontages, as far as I could see, but these seem to incorporate much else besides. Otherwise, there are cob cottages, and the prevailing timbering is cruck construction. It works, but there are limitations on span and height. The load is carried to the ground by the timbers, so the walls are there for weatherproofing. I remembered seeing some up at Old Sarum, but not, I think, when I was an even younger man in Ely. It seemed to me that much of the oak used here was probably scantling, so there must be a shortage of old woodland. All that time I had spent watching the new framing being put together in Salisbury may have been wasted. I had been itching to learn about the new long tenon joints I had seen that you can do with prefabricated frames, but it seemed that was not to be. New techniques are evolving all the time.

Was I now in the wrong place again, at the wrong time?

I don't drink heavily at all, but I discovered they do have good cider in Devon, so I spent an evening or two in a tavern, trying to get my ear attuned to local voices, before I began talking to some of the workmen around me. I was already feeling a little uneasy because each day I had scoured the streets of Exeter and two of the villages outside, looking for examples of local timber-framing.

I knew I had much to learn, so better get on with it. Perhaps furniture instead? Chins were rubbed and pints bought. The consensus came down in favour of trying, "that awful old chap who looks out onto the river. What's his name again?" They all agreed he was undoubtedly one of the very best craftsmen. But even as customers they seemed to give him a wide berth. "If you have staying power, there's probably no one better, but then no one has ever been with him for more than a few months." I may need someone to talk to in the evenings if he was that bad, I thought: "Do have some more cider… "

Jeffrey, he was called. He did indeed live near the lovely river, but his own home was ramshackle and not in any state I would have wanted mine to be, so my lodgings don't bear description. He was hard, and the kind of drinker that I could never be, but grudgingly I admit he was good at his work. I learned a great deal from him about wood of all kinds and how to choose the best available. He said he was interested in the new timber-framing in Salisbury. "Might try some here", he mumbled, "if I can get that oak."

We constructed cruck buildings with their matched curved timbers, and we made good furniture that he sold at cost price to the poor and at extortionate prices to the rich. I was never sure we were supposed to be doing both, but no one seemed to question Jeffrey. "That's how things are," he always said. The trouble was he looked like such an old ruffian, few rich people came to enquire, so many opportunities were lost. I don't remember ever having an evening to myself to drink cider in a tavern.

Jeffrey had a daughter who was quiet and downcast most of the time. He did not allow Jone to do any cleaning in his cottage, only to cook and to tidy up. I admit she intrigued me, and I tried hard to make her laugh. When her face lit up, she was so lovely that I lived for those moments. The old man knew how I felt and told me it was no good because her mother had died of some wasting disease, and he knew she was going the same way. I promised to look after her, to give her everything she needed if only he would allow me to marry her.

"Time you learned to read and write in English. Proper English. None of that foreign stuff, or how will you be able to do my accounts and write out contracts for the customers?

"My father was in the Baltic trade starting out, then some of the foreign ports got too hot for him, so I don't come from around here, nor speak local neither. We ended up in Exeter when I was a boy. I would rather have been with my grandfather, but I am used to it here now."

One hour after work, every night: "Learn your letters. Here they are, written out." He handed me a dirty old piece of parchment. "Reading first. We'll have two evenings together practising the sounds. Then writing, but that comes later. Get working. Here is most of The Owl and the Nightingale. I'm an owl. You won't forget that. That's all I've got." Wherever did he get it? He had a strong hand that I thought I recognised, so it looked like something he had copied out himself. "Get on with it then. You'll be writing something for me by next year."

Every single night, learning by myself. I was allowed one candle. Jone would sit with me, but never distract me, so it was my concentration that earned me her radiant smile. Or two hours on Sundays if I hadn't progressed sufficiently. He decided how to measure 'sufficiently', of course. It was many months before I read that poem all through–sharp, rude, and funny; it seemed to suit him. Perhaps there was more to Jeffrey than I knew.

For five years I slaved away for him in that joyless work place; my only respite, a longed-for (supervised) hour with Jone each Saturday, when we sat and gazed at the river. I had abandoned my little brother, so perhaps I didn't deserve any better. I wanted to learn. I wanted to learn everything. I dressed up and he put on an old hat when we attended the Gild meetings together, and after that minimum five-year period he admitted then that I was good enough to become a journeyman–otherwise I think he thought he would lose me. I would now be earning proper wages, and I knew that first I needed to save enough to buy all my own good tools.

"Here you are," he growled as he emptied out a filthy cloth bag with various items in it, among them a marvellous adze, saw, router, auger, and several different knives. "More of my grandfather's tools. You deserve them."

What a strange old creature he was. I say that, but looking at him properly, I don't think he was as old as he appeared to be. It was total self-neglect that had taken its toll. Jone was surely not yet twenty, so this must all have happened perhaps in the last fifteen years or so. First despair, then acceptance of it, then reject the world and hide away from it. Even then I hoped I wasn't going to be looking back at myself in those terms one day.

Part Two
THE JOURNEYMAN

Marry Jone if you want," Jeffrey said. "Then you can make her a coffin, not me. That's how things are." It used to set my teeth on edge, but that was his favourite phrase, for these days he accepted whatever life brought him. Some of his foibles made me shudder. He had a habit of running his awl in rings around the good board he had made for the trestles, until the grooves grew wide or narrow with and against the grain, but also deep, I couldn't get the crumbs of stale bread and dirt out of them when I was trying to clean up. He had started on the third one towards the centre when I became a journeyman. Scrubbing was just another one of the tasks I gave myself as I couldn't bear all the layers of grime.

Jeffrey did have some good qualities. One of them was that he was never vindictive. As a journeyman, I married Jone with his blessing, and we lived on his bit of land in a shack he gave us. I must call it that, because it wasn't any better, but the view we had across the river was beautiful.

He still expected us to be with him every day so Jone could make us all a meal. When we were alone, she was utterly transformed, and I loved her so much, my Jone. I hid from myself the fact that her skin was becoming translucent, and she was thin, oh so thin, despite the fact she carried my son. He was born some months later, and only a year after that I buried her, as her father had predicted.

Then Ned was all I lived for. He still is. We were out playing in the woods one day when he was two, chasing sunbeams, as I recall. A troop of horsemen came crashing through the trees and Ned was trampled. A quick backward glance, and then nothing. No one stopped. I had been in the wrong place again. I gathered afterwards, although I can't prove it, that they could have been the men who had come to collect the records in the Archa chest, so the documents for the loans the Exeter Jews had made could be examined.

Miraculously, he lived, my boy. His head hideously damaged outwardly, at least, and his left side hurt, and mangled, especially his leg. But his grandfather and I cared for him, for he was a fighter, my little son. I could not have worked at all had Jeffrey not helped me. He never complained and he allowed me to do most of the work that came in.

By this time, I had taken out a small loan from the Jews because I had spotted an opportunity in the market. Old Amiot, whom I found on the High Street and who agreed to the loan, had unexpectedly also sent a physician to see Ned. What had happened had not gone unnoticed in Exeter, and people were very kind to us.

I was told the city had one of the smaller Jewish communities within the system that old Archbishop Hubert Walter had set up before I was born. They were lucky it was so far away from the mainstream. Salisbury didn't have one at all of course, because it wasn't even there then, and Old Sarum was probably too small and too inconvenient for anyone. Hubert Walter himself would have known; he had nominally been bishop up at Old Sarum at some point.

Devonians only seem to get upset if there is none of their good cider around, or if you try to hurry them; they don't hate foreigners just because that is the easy thing to do when the king wants their money, and therefore yours as well, if you have borrowed some of theirs. They and the Jews there lived peaceably, side by side. Some of the wicked things that have happened in the larger cities, when mobs get whipped up, don't bear thinking about.

Each of their loan transactions is overseen by a Christian and a Jewish chirographer, with the documentation in three parts, with one part being kept in the local Archa chest. Jews were organised to settle in established towns, for their own safety as much as for the ease of administration, but small groups do exist in the countryside. Officially, there hadn't been any Jews living in England in Saxon times, even if occasionally one or two had found their way here, so this was William the Norman's idea, to invite them over here from Normandy when he needed to borrow money. By the time I knew anything about it, obviously it was more profitable to tax them harshly too. These Jews were much more sophisticated in the money markets than us, and usury was not forbidden to them as it is to Christians. The idea was that the king owned them directly, and then he could tax them at the same time as he would promise to 'protect' them, as far as I could see.

The opportunity I had seen was obvious to me. Fashionable people wanted houses and furniture built from old ships' timbers. There were plenty of those available and reasonably priced at that time, and these foolish people were eager to pay a premium. We know it is better if joints are formed from green timbers if they are to meld together to fit snugly, but some people always think they know better than you do.

I stayed a journeyman. I never bothered with the special piece of work the Gild would demand of a Master. I knew what I wanted to do and that was to look after my little boy. Anyway, one day I knew I would go home.

I always kept enough money back so I could repay my loan to them if it was called in because the Jews were taxed–fleeced even–by the king, without warning. I just used it as capital to invest in timber. I think I gathered that if a loan was called in and neither I nor the lender could pay, then I would owe that money to the king. Heaven forbid! I don't know how they coped. Their documentation was impeccable, and I never had any trouble.

✝

It was in July 1236, soon after all this had happened, when Mistress Elfrida turned up in Exeter from Salisbury, the last place she had visited. She brought with her a quantity of medicines and a small Jewish boy, coming to live with his uncle. His parents had been murdered in Norwich, apparently, where she lived. The visit itself was the cause of a lot of gossip, because here was a cross, tired old lady, only making a courtesy call on the bishop before she went to the Jewish community with all those salves and potions. At the time I had no idea who she was; I had no idea even that the Master had a sister. I didn't make that connection until many years later.

I was standing by the roadside after a visit to a new customer, as Amiot had told me to be there at that time. She saw me and whispered something to her companion. She just said, "Wait there," to me. I heard one, then another hour bell before I saw her walking towards me again. She hadn't had time to change as her clothes were still covered in dust from the road.

I had left Ned with his grandfather, who I knew cared for him as lovingly as I did, although the filthy conditions in his cottage were a great worry. I persuaded Jeffrey to come to my shack whenever I had to go to work out a price for a job. The old man always agreed, for he accepted what had happened to Ned much more readily. "That's how things are," he said, as he took Ned from me. Carrying a small boy to a new customer didn't lend you much credibility.

Elfrida and I walked in silence to my home, where Ned and his grandfather were. She ignored us both and went straight to Ned, holding his head and his poor body in turn and feeling his neck and down his back.

"My remedies are all herbal. If he is in pain, give him only two drops of this liquid in his milk, but never more than twice a day. The open wound on his head needs this lotion with a white dash on the flask. Use it very sparingly and cover it lightly with this gauze. Turn him frequently to stop him getting sores. This black dash lotion I am giving you is special; I don't have a lot of that. I am leaving you a flask to help keep his joints supple until he has more movement. Be very sparing with it. It will help when they ache as well. Eventually he should do some simple exercises, but before he learns how to do them himself, you must move his limbs gently for him." I asked her how well she thought he would recover.

She was honest: "I don't know", she said, "how much damage has been done to his head. It is far too early to say. His neck and his back seem alright to me, just badly bruised. His shoulder is torn, I think. Keep that still for now, but he should mend if you help him do the exercises and use my lotion. Use it on his leg too, but that is in a worse state, I'm afraid. Be very careful with that knee when you move him.

"His hands are not damaged, so he needs to use them. His right eye is certainly alright, so my suggestion would be to also help him at least to recognise colours. Are you also a wood-turner? Could you make him some little wooden cups, each of which you could colour differently?

"Whatever it is you are doing for the sick, always boil and cool any water you use first. You should do that for yourself, anyway. I'll call in again before I leave in two days' time."

Her voice was much softer now: "You look after your boy well, Mister Woodman. I'll ask Amiot to send his physician again. He will explain the simple exercises to you if I haven't had time." She nodded to Jeffrey, "Grandfather", she said.

What a wonderful old lady. Where on earth did she learn about such things? No bloodletting, no frog-skin paste, or dried bats' bellies pressed into open sores or anything else we dread and do not understand.

Woodman. I liked the sound of it, and resolved to adopt Woodman as my name when I returned home.

✝

I stayed in Exeter for two more years, until after old Jeffrey had died. He died, I am afraid, from blood-poisoning, the great fear that stalks every carpenter.

A few days after Mistress Elfrida left Exeter, he had suddenly said, "We had better get a nurse in for Ned. My sister will come. Never had any children of her own. She'll be good enough with him." I had no idea he had any relations. Why didn't she come to our wedding? "Best not", he had said when I couldn't stop myself asking him. That's what they say around here. Did she live nearby? I wondered vaguely if she was anything like Jeffrey.

Jeffrey's sister turned up only three days later. She lived not too far away in fact, only across the other side of the city. I was astonished.

"Our father was a sea captain", he said, by way of not much explanation at all. "Her mother was from a Turkish tribe in Anatolia. He brought both of them back very soon after my mother had died. He hardly noticed me; I was still away at the school. She doesn't approve of me. I can't think why. She never married, couldn't find anybody rich enough, I expect. She wouldn't live here–thank goodness–because we're not smart enough, but she has said she'll come every day if we need her to keep Ned clean and fed. I don't think she is in the best of health herself, mind you."

It occurred to me that I hadn't even wondered how it was that Jeffrey could read and write. He would have learned Latin first and foremost, of course. His mother ill, and dying, his father away at sea with at least one other wife and child in a far-off country. Of course he was sent away to school, and probably had to live there most of the time. Schools are hard places. His childhood doesn't bear thinking about.

She had a face like dough, as Jeffrey had, but she had glittery blackcurrant eyes and, above her wheezing chest, she wore a gold necklace somewhere in the folds of her chin. She was kind enough to Ned but her lack of empathy and inexperience with children showed. She was rather sparse with the affection and rough with the lotions, so I did all that in the evenings. Her cooking was also a bit dubious, so Jeffrey and I muddled along ourselves. I asked what her name was. She said, "Rini", I think. I'll never know why he hadn't mentioned her before, but I guessed that in the past it had involved a falling out with his father. Other people's lives are unknowable; I have enough trouble with my own.

✝

Jeffrey's foot had turned bad suddenly, shortly after some wood he was cutting splintered, and he had suffered a serious cut from his saw that he had dropped on it. He died mercifully quickly. He didn't seem to have much money because of his warped generosity. I sold up for him afterwards, keeping a portion of what he had left me for Ned, and I stuffed the Poor Box in the cathedral church full. I included some of the coins and three unpaid promissory notes I had found hidden under his mattress. The canons could have those too and chase them up, as hopefully they would have been from the rich people who supported them and would now want to save face. They could benefit instead of this impecunious old man.

Angrily, I scrubbed his trestles and the gouged-out board, with its three irregular tracks now complete. I just hoped they would acknowledge in their prayers that it was Jeffrey who had given them this gift, and not his debtors. The board and trestles were coming with me, a memory of him, shall we say. I even had to wipe away a tear because I knew we had grown quite fond of each other in some strange, unfathomable way.

I didn't need the money. It wasn't mine, and anyway I had saved enough myself to start my own business. Rini just shrugged her shoulders and stayed in her own home. Once, I had gone to have a peek at where she lived; it was all much too smart for us, as Jeffrey had said. They must have wondered at the cathedral church whatever had happened the day I left–if they ever managed to get the key in the lock of the Poor Box to open it.

It wasn't that I didn't like Exeter, but the memories were all too painful for me. The trouble was also that I had always known where my real home was. No, not Ely, but Salisbury, that most unlikely boggy field with its mad bishop; that lovely, new, and hopeful place.

Jeffrey had a horse and cart, which I supposed were now mine. I hired two servants to help me take Ned into Wiltshire. I could see it was going to be a long and difficult journey. The story of my life, I had thought bitterly. Somehow, I had to put Ned on the two mattresses and safely pack around him, Jeffrey's board and trestles and my belongings that I was taking with me. Ned's mother's smile was in my head always, so she didn't take up any room in the cart. I had already been down to the quay to buy a waterproof covering for it all.

I had never moved back into Jeffrey's wreck of a home. For one thing it would have taken too much scrubbing and scraping to clean it up to any standard a prospective buyer would consider. I decided to abandon it and let it fall, to return to the earth from which it had come. It seems to me there is nothing wrong in doing that. Let someone come and find the land and build a new life there. What a romantic fool I am. Adjacent landowners would now squabble over it for years to come. There was no documented ownership that I had found, or I would have stuffed that in the Poor Box as well. Perhaps he had torn up anything not written in English.

I had remained in the shack Jone and I had shared because that was where the good memories were. Her merry face as I tripped over that broken flagstone yet again, her warmth as we lay on the bracken and wool mattress we had salvaged and restuffed with wool we had gathered from the hedgerows, before we laughingly gave up and bought some from the market.

No, no-one would want this old shack, so greedily I knew all those memories would always be mine, only mine. Jeffrey had one or two foreign religious pictures tucked away, and a carved ivory and some objects made from amber. Amber I could recognise. Those were what I sold for Ned, and for a surprising amount of money.

As I was preparing to leave, with Ned already tucked in a corner of the cart with a bale of straw to protect him from jolts and falling furniture, I heard a clip-clop up the road and Amiot's son-in-law was who he said he was, appeared with a small horse-drawn litter for my boy. It needed two horses, so one of his servants could accompany us, he said.

I had never thought of such a thing, I was so used to living with very few worldly goods. I couldn't stop my eyes misting over. We bowed to each other in the chill morning air, as he gave the reins that he was holding to one of his servants. I had never met this man before and the kindness overwhelmed me. We shook hands as I lingered and said awkwardly that all the servants would return with the litter as soon as possible. He touched Ned's forehead before melting away into the side streets.

The number of Jews was dwindling in Exeter, but there, in that civilised and rather remote city, they had escaped much of the hatred so often stirred up by those who owe them money. The king never seems to leave them alone though, and they are an obvious target. He is always after more and more tax money in the form of 'tallage' from them to fund his wars. He 'owns' these people, you see. He is their direct liege lord. They must pay him all this money in return for his 'protection'. There must be a word for that. What do I know? I am, after all, just an observer.

†

I arrived back home here in Salisbury as Mister Woodman, without a clue about where I should be. We stayed at an inn a mile or two outside. Another traveller asked me what I did, and I said I was a woodman. "You'll be going up to the framing place then?"

"Yes," I agreed, "I would." Of course, I would. Why hadn't I thought of that? So, the next day we diverted across the fields, and I came upon a derelict cottage. I was used to such living conditions. Mine, I thought. I had been told in which direction we should go to find the framing place.

The framing place with its sawpit was a little further on. Leaving Ned in his litter with the servants, I dropped down to the large sawpit, where I was told someone called Bernie should be.

I saw the hat first. The considerable rest of him was hidden behind neatly stacked piles of oak and elm. "I'm sorry to disturb you," I said. "I'm looking for someone called Bernie, but your hat appears to be the only person here." He roared with laughter. "I could do with some help," he said, "Short of everything here, we are."

I could work here, I thought. It was like arriving in Heaven. I am fairly small and wiry, and Bernie was a man-mountain made of muscle, but I liked him immediately. He wasn't any taller than me and he wore this ancient-looking felt hat that flopped down almost as far as his huge, broad smile. I'm sure you get the picture.

Possibly, he liked me as much as I liked him at that moment. I told him I had money to invest as well as my skills and my time, "as soon as I have made a home for my injured son, Ned." I said I must go back to the track to fetch him, and to pay everyone for all the trouble they had taken to get us here, along with enough to pay for their accommodation on the return journey.

"I'll help you," said Bernie, following. I gave Jeffrey's horse to one of my servants who looked as though he would treat her well. The other two were given extra silver pennies. We shook hands and they all left, trundling along with the litter, well satisfied. Bernie took them to the edge of the field and showed them a track that would be easier for them. Bernie then very gently took Ned from me, as soon as he returned. He laid him down so carefully on the mattresses by the bale of straw, saying: "You're home now, young man." He told me that the cart with its cover would be quite safe there, until we needed to unload it.

Bernie indicated a stretch of land between the pit and the framing place. This was where he stored the matched timbers. "The pile there, look. The timbers are all marked up on that little cottage, so we had better make a start on the footings." I looked at the ground and at the sun, asking him if his hall was facing due east and west, so one set of shutters could always be closed against a prevailing wind. "Just slightly west-south-west is best here, I would think", he said. He would know.

I emptied my tool bag on the ground; I suppose I wanted him to know I meant business. He saw the tools Jeffrey had given me, as well as the ones I had inherited from him, and he gave a low whistle. "Very nice indeed". I put the old man's beautiful trestle saw down last, very reverently on the ground. His smile grew even wider. It was more than enough for his seal of approval. I suppose it was then we knew we had become partners. Over the next two weeks we became workmates, but by then we were also the best of friends.

He lived very close by. On that first day he took me a short way down the curved track and pointed out his own cottage. It seemed large to me, and I couldn't think Ned and I would need a home as big as that. We slept on our mattresses on his great hall floor that night, but the next morning he appeared before I was dressed and said, "I'm big and strong. If I came to your cottage every morning about this time, or whenever you think is best, I could carry Ned to the privy. The rest of the time he can use this pottery bottle with a big neck. Will that do?"

Oh Bernie, the endless months I have struggled with it all and as Ned grows heavier, often failed. I didn't know God had angels in felt hats who look like you.

"Where would you like to live? There aren't any other people this far over. How about here? Or here?" He pointed to some more ground. "Over there, look, you could have a nice garden if we included that stand of trees as well. I suppose all this is my land. Just got no money, you see. There's an underground stream, so you can share my well."

I used to lie in bed at night, often unable to believe that such good fortune had come my way. I reminded myself to ask Bernie if this was one or two burgage plots he had, because it seemed so large. I was a free man too, so I wouldn't have to apply for a licence to trade, nor pay market tolls. Life was harder for the un-free, even in towns. Bernie was a professional carpenter to the very end of his fingertips. No apprentice would ever dare produce shoddy work here, yet he was so kind and gentle with Ned. He kept thanking me for allowing him to share in his upbringing, because he had no children of his own.

Ned and I lived up by the framing place, quietly and unobtrusively for many years. There were squirrels and rabbits and drifts of wildflowers, and such peace. When we had started to build, right from the morning of the second day, Ned sat in the hedgerow, leaning against an alder tree, watching all the activity with great interest–well that is what I told myself anyway. As we progressed with our new home, two of Bernie's men came to help us from time to time when there was a lull in trade. Bernie then brought an old wheelbarrow along for Ned to sit in. He had stuffed it with cushions, so we could both talk to him as we worked. Bernie didn't seem to be the sort of person who would have feather-filled cushions; I only learned about Mabel later. We slept on Bernie's floor meanwhile, in such bizarre surroundings, but I'll save that for later too.

I told Bernie my whole story. He was a good listener, and frankly it was such a relief to unburden myself. He even asked me to describe Jone to him because he thought it would help, and it did because it made her real again and I could share with him who she was, as well as her loveliness. He asked me why I had done nothing about the soldier whose horse had trampled Ned. I didn't realise I had tears running down my face as I answered him. He stopped me, and said: "I know, I don't think there is any justice for the likes of us. I'm sorry, I won't mention it again. Here, you take my kerchief."

Bernie never said a word about any of this to anyone. He heard from a customer one day when the Master had died, and I risked going down to the cathedral church to say thank you for looking after Joseph for me. I had to, but I felt so inadequate. It was all I could do. I saw that he had finished the crossing before he died, and I am glad of that for him. I am a mere traveller, like everyone who has come here, gazing upon all that has been done.

Ned has been talking to us the best he can for a few years now. We understand everything he says and his speech improves all the time. These days he always joins in when I play my little flute and sing him songs from my childhood. He first did that when his voice was beginning to break, I remember, when he sounded like a corncrake with a croup.

We improved and enlarged the framing place and the sawpit and took on several more carpenters. Bernie lorded it over everyone, in and out of the pit, and I ran the business. Thank you, Jeffrey, for my training. To everyone else who came up there I was known as "Woody" Woodman. Only Bernie knew my real name.

I have just re-read this piece. Was I really thinking I could sweep so many years under the nearest bush, and not tell you anything more? Here I am, ashamed of myself again.

†

Before I tell you about meeting my new friends, or about how difficult it can be to know how to help people when you are out of your depth, I'll tell you a little about the sort of lives Bernie and Ned and I had here, while Ned was growing from a child into a young man. Even just writing that, I realise all over again how long a period that is, as much as my first ten years here as a stonemason and all the time I lived in Exeter put together.

This little cottage that we have made our home, suits us. Thanks to Mistress Elfrida, I knew from his earliest years that bright colours would be important to Ned. Everything about our home is bright and cheerful. One of the first things I did was to collect some sawdust and mix it with fillers and glue, but not before I had sent Bernie to the market to buy at least three different pigments. I filled the three rings of uneven gouges right around Jeffrey's board. Go on Jeffrey, you would love it! You would love it, Jeffrey, because you wanted your grandson to be happy. Don't think I don't know that.

The thin inner ring is bright blue, thin because Jeffrey had to stretch his arms to get that far, the middle one is green and the big, even more wobbly outer one is red, which is Ned's favourite colour. Sanded down and polished, the whole thing is incredible. Ned has his own place to sit, which is where the red line is widest and collides with the green one and where Bernie then painted a big smile on the blue line for him. This is how we mean to live here.

Bernie's hobby is model making, but we'll come to that shortly. His cottage is different to ours. Now, when he isn't safely in his kennel, it includes The Bailiff, the old growling guard-dog he always thought he needed. Bernie looks after that dog well enough, even when he is snarling at him, but he won't be replaced. Before I came and when people owed Bernie money, he said he used to say he would send in The Bailiff to encourage them to pay up. They knew he didn't mean it. Ned is most unsure about that dog!

When Ned had just turned six, Bernie made him a set of twelve wooden cubes. They are smooth and lovely with rounded corners and all different colours. He often plays with them on our board. I never knew how much he understood. Sometimes we put down one, and said "one", then two and so on. One day there were four on the table. Bernie and I were talking as well as playing. I said "four", but Bernie had taken one away. I had said "four" without seeing what had happened, and Ned put it back again. Bernie and I looked at each other. I added a cube and said "five". Bernie took one away, and Ned, yes Ned, said "four". His first thought-out word: two grown men, crying with joy.

He understood. He couldn't manage all the sounds properly then, but we had hope, you see, and we were well-rewarded.

I am afraid Ned's left leg was always going to be useless, although later he could put it on the ground. I made him some splints, but he didn't like them. He used Bernie as a "pit prop" when he was old enough and strong enough to stagger with him to the privy. One eye was damaged as well as the left side of his face. He has Jone's wavy hair. He was better sitting down, but he couldn't get up from the ground without help. How we loved him. He sat in the garden with me, on a high back stool I made for him, and directed operations. He still likes growing carrots and tickling my nose with their green ferny tops.

Bernie used to do all the market shopping. Living in Salisbury, it was easy of course. We always say there was nothing you couldn't buy on our market.

Bernie knew the best stalls for pies, and for meat and fish and bread. His basket was linen-lined, and I washed out the linen cloths that covered fresh food on its plate each time. I dried our own peas and beans, or they came from the grocer. I grew our fresh vegetables. My cooking was a bit primitive, just a big iron trivet and plate for searing meat and cooking fish over the fire, and a big and a small pot for potage, and another for water. Until I built a separate kitchen, that is. It was still a bit primitive even after that, but we did have a spit for meat then. The dairyman calls with milk and cheese, and we make our own butter in a shaker. I never conquered bread, but I am still thinking about it. There are plenty of good bakers in the city. Bernie's cooking arrangements are even simpler than mine, so I often prepare enough for three.

Someone at the market makes our clothes from measurements we send. Bernie also heard of this wonderful lady who sewed bed covers with cut-out stars, at her house. He put in an order for one for Ned, the wool cloth and silver tissue, sewn with cut out stars all over it. It was perfect. It was only later I found out who she was, this needlewoman of great renown, and finder of the best linen sheets! Another day he came back with some tooth-cleaning powder that her friend made, and little squares of linen with which to apply it. Yes, I said. Buy more–it will keep. Having teeth pulled is really horrible. Bernie likes honey, although we know it's not good for your teeth, so next time he bought up her whole weekly supply of tooth powder from her bread stall, and a special loaf as well, for which he had to join a long queue.

Fear of becoming ill was our greatest worry; it always is. I have Ned to look after, and my knowledge of anything beyond prayer and a dock-leaf is minimal. I dislike the thought of physicians, and of barber-surgeons even more, and I keep telling myself it wasn't just because I was a coward. A lot of people grew herbs, I knew that, but I didn't know much about them. Time for Bernie to find out when Mabel, his lady friend, came. Once, I had heard her talk about her own herb garden. I knew about peppermint, so we drink the infusion all the time. How I would have liked that old lady in Exeter to step this way for an hour or so.

†

Eventually, Bernie gave me a good talking to. Why was I still lurking up here after ten years? Apart from masons, there could be hardly anyone left who would have known me, and anyway there were so many more people here now to get swallowed up in. And I had that horrible beard. We had an apprentice who was steady and a nice lad, he'll have looked after younger brothers, Bernie was sure:

"We can ask him to sit with Ned from time to time. His name is Jonathan and if you want some new shoes, you can damn well go down there and choose the leather yourself."

He was right, of course. I agreed to go down there only if he could find me a floppy felt hat that fitted me from the stall on the market where he said he had bought his, long ago, and if it came down over my face as far as his hat did. I agreed that Jon was indeed alright. Ned just laughed and laughed at my hat, so it was all worth it. Not very often, but from time to time thereafter, I went into the city in disguise, in my floppy hat and sporting my straggling beard. What a sight I must have looked.

Jon carved a little wooden bird for Ned. It had wings that went up and down. Ned was fascinated. He was fifteen going on sixteen by then, and very curious. He examined the bird for hours and moved the wings slowly, then faster and faster:

"How fly?" he would say. When we were in the garden one sunny day later in the week, he pointed to a chaffinch, and told me it was, "like mine." I used to muse from time to time on what he might have done, if only… But I always heard a familiar voice in my head: "That's how things are."

"Yes, Jeffrey," I always silently replied.

It was on such a day, when Ned and I were in the garden, that we heard Bernie pounding up the track, a good deal faster than usual. We went to the gate, and we could see he had some news of great importance: "We have a place, we really do. I can hardly believe it. We have come up in the world!" He was hanging onto my gate post by this time, out of breath.

"Bernie, what are you talking about?"

He took a great gulp of air: "Mistress Tubby," said my delighted friend, "*Washerwoman to The Clergy*, has graciously given us a set day and a time each week that must be strictly observed of course, because her drying racks are so full. Isn't that wonderful? I did say we were woodworkers, so we needed to be extra clean. She is the best. No more spreading my linen on the bushes for all to see." Even Ned was trying not to laugh.

Bernie's cottage was, and still is, full of oak and leather. "It makes me feel safe," says the man-mountain. The best oak we know of around here is from Chippenham. Of course, we both need leather for our work, for good strong boots and tool wraps and long wrist guards, but his seating is all leather covered as well.

I think I have said already that the thing that terrifies woodworkers is a splinter. If you don't see it go in and it turns bad, you could die just as quickly as Jeffrey did, because your blood can become poisoned. It is that simple. Every woodworker should have his fine long tweezers like every scribe has his knife, and hopefully someone to extract the splinters gone in too far, and the ones that you can't reach. Apart from Jeffrey, woodworkers are also very clean. You don't want the oil and dirt from your hands staining the pale new wood. You can buy something on our market with which to treat cuts, Bernie says, because you hope and pray you don't ever need to go anywhere near a barber-surgeon.

I digress. Bernie's hall is much bigger than ours because it accommodates two rivers and his models: a castle with a drawbridge and a moat (that drawbridge never did go up and down properly), and at the other end, an abbey, and a flood plain. The nights we slept there on our mattresses; I remember we had to move the floodplain over a bit.

Bernie comes from near Tewkesbury. His father had been a real woodman, doing coppicing. I am guessing, but Bernie seems to have spent a good deal of his childhood roaming the forests with his father. Wood was his life, wood his being. He needed to hold it, and wanted to work on it way beyond coppicing, which he said was for beginners in loving wood. He had an uncle who was a bit better heeled than his father, and it was he who paid for Bernie's apprenticeship as a carpenter.

There is a lot of water in and around Tewkesbury apparently, and Bernie took first to making rafts and then building a small boat for his uncle, who said he would help him set up in business. But where? They had heard of the new city being built. Salisbury would obviously be ripe for timber-framing, and a new cathedral church was being built on water meadows. It was that last bit that caught Bernie's attention.

You may be wondering, is Bernie haunted by water? It's not panic, but water enters his every calculation. Whenever he wants to play with his models, he can't have a fire because there would be so much water around, it would put it out. He always brings the water into his hall in two huge leather buckets and several big jugs.

Now, if the moat ever overflows into the rivers that are in the channel he has dug out and lined all around the circumference of the interior of his central hall (the side on your right as you go in being the Avon, with the side on your left, the Severn), it sometimes spills over quite seriously as far as the floodplain. If that happens, when his rivers are too full of the water from the moat that Bernie is still pouring water into as well, then there would be a knock on our door, and I would have to go over there quickly to bale him out, while he dries off in front of my fire and plays with Ned. I think this must be a different Avon to ours; "bigger and mightier" is how Bernie describes it.

His models are all made in elm and white birch-wood and are a work of art. People don't quite believe that Bernie is like he is, but I wouldn't change my best friend in any way. He thinks his hometown may have a problem with water, he says, and he would love to solve it for them.

I don't think there has ever been an official Mistress Bernie. He does have his Mabel, who was an old childhood friend, but not quite as large as him. She arrives under full sail from spring to autumn, three times a year. She comes up the track, huffing and puffing and swinging her bag and waving cheerily. I asked Bernie once how she got here. He just winked at me. I bet he hires a wagon from someone in the city to fetch her from Tewkesbury and drop her off, just before she reaches this track of ours.

Her visits cheer Bernie immensely, until she sighs and says after a few days, or at the most a week, no, she can't stand all that water and those models and that awful old hat as well as The Bailiff, and she would rather stay a widow, thank you. They always part on good terms and know that she will be back another time. "Good old Bailiff," Bernie says, after he has waved her farewell. Mentally, I had marked an extra day for her next visit, when Bernie and I could attend a class that she would give us on the uses of all the herbs she knew about, before she took one of us, hopefully me, to the market in our hat to buy some plants. Bernie is no gardener. Also, I wondered if she could help me with a recipe for honey cake. I must be doing something wrong. I bake it on the griddle, but the honey always runs out of the bottom. "It doesn't matter," said Bernie. "Stop fussing. It's lovely. Look at Ned's face when he is trying to lick it off his elbow."

So, have I caught him out? What will he do when The Bailiff dies? Mabel may then think perhaps she could cope with models and the floods and agree to one of his frequent proposals of marriage. He would have to think of something else, very fast!

The more I see of Mabel, the more I like her. She told me she could plant herbs in Bernie's garden, as long as I would promise to look after them. At one time, I gather, they had known each other quite well, but her father had married her off to a boatman. Mabel wasn't the right shape to go in boats, but other women were. One day, one of them was sufficiently incensed to chase this boatman with a fish slice she had been wielding in the galley, when he slipped on some guts on the deck and fell and hit his head.

It had been an accident; Mabel kept the cottage and gave the woman the boat. But by that time Bernie had moved to Salisbury, acquired The Bailiff and was making his models. She enjoys coming to see him, but his accoutrements are beyond her. I plucked up courage once to ask her what he looked like when he took off his hat. "He doesn't," she said, "as far as I can see."

"Not ever?" I ventured. I'm sure she blushed. I should have left it there.

"Not ever..." she said slowly and meaningfully, "...as far as I can see."

Ned liked Mabel too. She always brought him a thoughtful present and stayed to play games with him. Very gradually I was widening the circle of people he knew and with whom he felt comfortable. Ned even allowed Mabel to wash his hair, which was something he had not allowed me to do for him for a while now.

I think Bernie instinctively felt the noose tightening around his neck. "I wish you would stop looking at me like that and not saying anything so loudly," he once said. "I have no intention of letting her get away, but meanwhile I have The Bailiff to look after, and I know I shall miss my models so much."

"Oh Bernie, you have plenty of room here, mate. I'll have the herb garden at my place, and couldn't we just attach another little hall with a hearth, at the side of yours?"

Bernie even lifted his hat to scratch his head in amazement: "Yes! Why on earth didn't I think of that?"

I must report that The Bailiff died at a great age, in his sleep, snarling happily to the end. He is buried to the side of Bernie's cottage, behind his old kennel. Bernie then asked me if I would write 'The Bailiff' for him on the kennel itself.

I had wondered from time to time whether I should suggest to Ned that we could have a dog. It always worried me that he would immediately think of The Bailiff, whom he only ever saw snarling in his kennel, because Bernie would not have dreamt of frightening him by having the dog in the cottage when Ned was there. It must be said that The Bailiff had never hurt anyone in all his life. He just sounded as though he would, Bernie had said, so he was the very best sort of guard dog. In fact, he thought perhaps he just had some sort of constriction in his nose or throat that made him sound so fierce all the time. He was happy enough, and enjoyed the early morning and late evening walks he had with his master, because that was the only time of day Bernie judged they wouldn't meet anyone else.

It was an unresolved conundrum until three winters past, when an old woman hobbled up here saying she had heard about Ned, and was there anything she could do? I sat her down quickly, because otherwise she looked as though she might fall down, and I brewed her some peppermint, of which she approved. She talked to Ned all the time, and he laughed and smiled at her. I marvelled at it, because this was someone he did not know and he would certainly not have done that, even just a year or two ago. She didn't ask my name because I expected someone had already told her, and she had left before I wondered whether I should ask who she was.

Several weeks later she was back, on a freezing cold day, carrying her shopping basket. "Here", she said, "a present for Christmas for Ned. One of the Yorkie masons called on me and said he and his colleague were soon going back to live in York, by Christmas he hoped, and did I know of anyone who could take the pup?" She opened one half of the hinged lid and a floppy-eared head appeared with two large brown eyes, under a bundle of woolly, cream curls. "He's called Nobbut," she said firmly. "When I asked the mason how he could ever give him up, he said, 'he's no' but a dog.' I hoped Nobbut wasn't listening to him! He told me another name, but I said no, and that Nobbut would do nicely, thank you. I think Nobbut and Ned will get on very well, don't you?"

The loveliest little pup you ever saw gazed around at all three of us and crawled out of that basket. I think I said something foolish, like "he must be some sort of spaniel". Nobbut looked at me reproachfully (*some sort of spaniel?*) and I had the distinct impression he was rather offended at my clumsy reference to his probable ancestry. He then looked back at the old lady and wagged his tail. He shook himself and went straight up to Ned on his daybed by the window. I had only thought of making that bed for him recently because he still can't get up from the floor on his own. Ned was smiling as he held out a hand. Nobbut put a paw on the cushions by his head. They gazed at each other, and that was that; there are no other words, just mutual life-long devotion.

Bernie arrived just as the old lady was leaving and said, "Mistress Annie Baker. Well! Well! A very good morning to you. I didn't know you knew about us here."

So, this was Mistress Annie Baker! She didn't recognise me as the errant brother who had come to see Joseph once or twice when he was ill, and I hadn't recognised the Master's good-looking housekeeper. She had always been completely swathed in her apron and wimple, but the years can be cruel. All I had to offer her were my profound thanks, and a slice of honey cake and a little pot of parsley Ned had planted up in the summer.

Part Three
TRAVELLING DAYS

I have delayed telling you about Vivie until now, because I hardly know how to start. It is so upsetting, because you see right at the beginning there was nowhere for Vivie to go to seek justice. I have never thought too much about this before; there should have been, of course there should have been.

All this that I am going to tell you happened nearly five years ago, but it will be imprinted on my mind, always. It was far too late by then.

In her absence, I am going to be writing this for you. Would she be horrified? Probably. But in her moments of lucid, searing honesty, she may well have said, "No, no, say more, more. I don't deserve any better." She deserves much better.

I may not have drawn a clear enough picture of where we are, near the framing place. The day I came here, when I had swerved off the track to follow a field path, I had come across a derelict cottage, nearer to the earth it had come from than even Jeffrey's old home in Exeter. Mentally, I had marked it out for where Ned and I would be living. Only about half a mile further on, however, I had come across Bernie and my new life and new home, altogether in one place, so I never had to give the derelict hovel another thought.

I looked on my own garden as a paradise and spent most of any spare time I had working in it. Bernie was almost always in the pit during daylight hours, sawing away and directing operations, or else he was here with Ned if I was needed at the framing place. Just occasionally when Jon came up to be with Ned for an hour or so, I went for a walk across the fields.

The tumbledown cottage was still there, not in any worse state of repair, so once it must have been basically sound. I walked past and picked a handful of poppies to take home for Ned. On my way back I thought I saw a shadow move inside, across what had once been a shuttered window, but I felt silly even calling out, "Hello", because there was complete silence. I went home. Ned and I arranged the poppies in a jug on the windowsill, and I thought I had forgotten all about what I believed I had imagined.

I hadn't though, because it must have been on my mind going to sleep that night. When he came up to our cottage first thing as usual, I asked Bernie if he would mind staying to have breakfast with Ned while I went back to have a look around. Bernie never minded staying for breakfast. He always knew if we had any potage left over, or where the eggs and the bread and the butter were kept.

I walked across the field again, always veering to the left at a certain point to avoid the place where a skylark nests each year. I think she has finished now until next spring, but I avoided it just in case. I could feel my boots soaking up the early morning damp. There was the cottage, which looked and felt entirely empty. I peered inside the broken-down door, just as the sun was slanting through the window I had seen yesterday.

There was no one there, of course. No fire had been lit, but it was late summer after all. I turned around to go back to the door and suddenly noticed an old stool. There was no dust on the top of it at all, even though the legs were covered in accretions. Then I looked more closely at a ledge in the corner, where there were some very withered poppies and cornflowers lying there, but as though they had been arranged and had fallen out of a pot. A woman then. The flowers must have been there for a fair while. I admit the hairs were standing up on my neck by this time, because I had seen no footprints around and had heard no sound.

I left everything as I had found it, but I laid two sets of thin crossed twigs across the threshold and went home.

The dairyman had been. Bernie had lit the fire and was waiting for the griddle to heat up. Ned was dressed and smiling, he held out his hands to me as I came in. Everything was as it should be. Perhaps my imagination had just run riot.

I told Bernie about the stool. "Kids?" he offered, "playing house?" Yes, I thought. It must have been. I returned once or twice as and when my work would allow, but usually when Jon looked in to say hello to Ned, or Bernie was there. "Won't be long", became a stock phrase. Sometimes the twigs were broken, and sometimes they weren't. I stopped worrying about it.

Then, one day, some weeks later, I had left Ned with Jon. He was no longer our apprentice of course, but one of our best and most trusted carpenters. He still liked to come to sit with Ned from time to time. It was a lovely day, so I took a short walk. As I was passing the cottage door, I saw some blackberries dropped outside. They looked freshly picked, so I peered inside and saw a bed of oak leaves laid on the stool with a pile of those blackberries on it, and a kerchief lying on the ground. Whoever had been here had brushed their sleeve against the rough doorpost because there was a snag of fine wool caught there.

"Halloo," I called out, "is everything alright?" There was a movement outside and a thin waif of a woman tried to dart away but left a poor broken shoe behind. "Don't worry," I said, "I'm not going to hurt you. Is that your dinner there?" She was wrapping herself now in some vast woollen garment, the same colour as the snag of wool on the doorpost. At least she wouldn't be cold as well.

Something made me ask if I could have a blackberry too. I felt in my bag and found, underneath the hazelnuts I had collected, some bread and cheese left over from the lunch-piece I had taken with me. She looked as thin as though she was starving. Her dark grey hair had escaped from whatever had held it, and her eyes were hollow. "We could have a proper meal, look–" I held out the piece of cheese.

She sat on the ground with only her bare legs and her face peeking out. "Yes," she agreed. "I do wish Maudie would come."

"Are you expecting Maudie too then," I asked.

"Oh no, Maudie is dead. The seagulls told me so. It was all so long ago now. She was my sister, and I loved her. I never loved anyone else. NO ONE," she suddenly shouted at me as she tried to get up.

"No, do come and sit down and have some of this cheese and some blackberries." I was out of my depth here already. I don't know why I asked her what the seagulls had said.

"They shrieked at me, MAUD haha ha ha ha. MAUD haha ha ha ha. MAUD ha ha ha ha. I knew then she had fallen in the harbour. They didn't know I called her Maudie, you see, and that she called me Vivie. So, they didn't know I was her sister when they were screaming and laughing."

"No, no, I'm sure they didn't, Vivie. Where was this and how long ago?"

"I am glad you are calling me Vivie, no one else does, not around here. She wanted to die, you know. We lived in Christchurch. Father had kept coming for her in the night, and mother pretended she didn't know. She did know; it was why she hit her. Maudie wanted to kill herself and the baby she said she would have, but she wanted me to run away because he would come for me next, and Maudie loved me. He was one of the men in charge of the shipwrecks off Poole harbour, but he stole some of the cargo too."

Her voice was suddenly lower, and she peered at me: "MAUD haha hah HA HA! They didn't know her, those seagulls, did they?

"I don't know why I am telling you this. You don't want anything from me, do you? I don't do that anymore since he gave me this," she said, cuddling into the garment and patting her arm. "Maudie gave me the coins she had found at home and said I had to run away quickly.

"I threw away the foreign ones because those would be the ones he had stolen, but I kept the others for my rent when I had found somewhere to live. Someone gave me a lift in a cart. I paid for that, you know. I ended up here and found a cottage to rent, but I didn't have very much money left. I hadn't found any work. I was quite pretty in those days, and I had to earn enough to eat." She was crying.

"All the women disliked me. I could hear the waves calling my name. The seagulls didn't know it, you see. BUT THE WAVES DID." I couldn't think what on earth she meant. I had to get her to safety, she was clearly out of her mind. "The waves only knew my real name too. Not Vivie. Only Maudie called me Vivie. I could hear it in my head as they lapped onto the sand and shingle and sucked it back into the sea. 'AhhhVeecesssse ', they said, 'AhhhVeecesssse '."

I stared at her, my throat suddenly very dry. Oh, Dear Lord, I had to stop her and get her home. AhhhVeecesssse? *That Avice.*

Everyone had heard of *That Avice*, Bernie had once said. A bad lot, long since retired. Once, she had lived around the corner from Mistress Annie Baker's shop and had entertained several men that Annie had known about.

Bernie didn't know all I know now, but he would know what to do. I'm sure we should find the friars. We should go to the friars. It was too far for her to walk over there with only one shoe. I helped her up and saw what she was wearing was a large woollen travelling cape of the finest quality. It was obviously very old, and rather moth-eaten.

"He gave me this," she said, "a priest, long ago. I was cold, so cold. My clothes weren't very good. I was ashamed of them, you know.

"I was outside the cathedral church when it was nearly dark, gazing at it. It sounds silly because that is what he was doing too. He must have seen it every day. I told him I couldn't go in there, even when it was finished because I was a sinner. They wouldn't want me in there, would they? He said of course they would. That can't be right, can it?

"He saw I was cold. He took off his cape. He said it had always been hidden away in a cupboard until it was needed. He had only just brought it out again. Look at the hood, isn't it lovely? Then he said that he didn't need it anymore. It had travelled a long, long way already, for justice. What is justice? The cape was only about memories for him now. He thought I needed it. It makes me feel like a good person, like Maudie."

I was beginning to feel very sick. I knew, I just knew. I don't know how I knew. He had helped my poor brother find his life. Was there another canon quite like him? This poor demented and tormented woman. The only person to help her was this man, perhaps when he himself was at death's door.

But what a man.

"I told him where I lived and he said he would give the friars enough money for my rent for a few weeks, and that they would help me, so I could stop doing it. He said he had nearly finished his own journeying here, and this travelling cape was now mine.

"He told me he wasn't giving away church property because they had owned the capes themselves, as they had both needed a disguise and this was brown, so you could walk in the trees outside in Canterbury and not be noticed. Wasn't that kind? And so clever. I wear it when I walk between the trees too when I come to find Maudie.

"I don't know who he was. I haven't sinned since, I never ever wanted to, anyway. So, I hide it away still and only wear it when I come out to find Maudie. No one knows I have it. But I am not allowed to tell you what my cottage is now, or the friars would be very cross." She put her fingers to her lips and said, "Shush."

I said, "When was this, Vivie?"

"A long time ago. It was winter you know and the next year all those people came from Yorkshire, so I never went down there again." She smiled at me, and I saw she had no teeth left. "I still live there, with others like me in the cottage now, and keep them safe. Some come and others go.

"Oh, I'm not supposed to tell you that. I really want to see Maudie again. You would like Maudie. I have told her I have this new house up here and she can come to care for me, because I know I am very ill now."

I wanted to shout out because of her pain. Yorkshiremen, the following year? Cold weather? That must have been late in 1244. I remembered Ned being ten, when he fell in a snowdrift and giggled because he couldn't get up. Bernie had told me when the Master had died, and that would have been not that long afterwards, with his memories, his own travelling days done, and this treasure of his already given away to begin another journey. Bernie had also said that the new bishop, a new master mason as well as the Master's replacement, with some more masons of their own, had all come down here from Yorkshire, after a spate of deaths.

"Shall I help you to my cottage, Vivie? I have some honey cake there. Do you like honey cake?"

"Oooh yes. I don't know, I don't remember."

I had been carefully guiding her along all this time. "There is my cottage, look".

Jon was outside with Ned. "Get Bernie quickly," I said, "and please come back yourself."

"Hello", she said to Ned, "I'm Vivie. How do you do? I don't do very well anymore. My shoe is broken. And it really hurts here, now." She was clutching her stomach. "They give me a liquid to drink. URRGH!" She spat on to the ground before taking off her cape. I took it from her and bundled it inside my door. Ned was holding on to the door post, but he had some Michaelmas daisies in his hand, which he held out to her. Oh, Ned!

Out of the corner of my eye, I could see Bernie and Jon hurrying towards me.

"Jon, take Ned inside please, one of us will be back soon."

"Bernie, can you bring the honey cake, and can we three go back to yours?"

I was making this up as I went along. How do we get her to the friars? Someone must look after Ned.

Bernie said. "Jon will look after Ned. Let's get her inside. If she talks to me, I will look after her while you go to find the friars." I was going to protest, but he said, "Just ask, they are always around. It must be you, because she needs help and neither Jon nor I know anything of what has happened, do we?"

I said yes, but then went home instead and asked Jon to run to the friary and stop the first friar he could find, ask him to go to Avice's cottage to find a pair of her shoes and then bring him up here, quickly.

"Just say she is very ill and unable to walk home because one of her shoes has broken. They will have a key to her cottage. Go now, please." I thought it through again, deciding that I had them around the wrong way. No matter, change clothes first.

Then I braced myself for something I thought I would never have to do. Bernie had always kept my hair short for me, but now I had to shave off my ragged beard; ragged because Bernie was so scathing about it that I had tried to hack it shorter from time to time.

I am fair-skinned, and my beard grew long and straggly rather than thick and bushy. I had a sharp razor because I needed to shave Ned very carefully each morning now. No time to wonder about it; Bernie could improve upon it tonight if needs be. We always had hot water bubbling over the fire.

Respectability was called for, very quickly. Best clothes, well, what passed for best clothes; those I used to wear to Gild meetings in Exeter, because Reginald of Ely had to be here before the friar came. The fastest transformation ever took place; I only cut my chin once. Tear a corner off a dock leaf to stop the blood. No good; try bread. Might find a cobweb between here and Bernie's. Then I put on my best clothes and found they still fitted me.

I put Ned in the wheelbarrow and wheeled him quickly down to Bernie's. Bernie came out and said "WHAT? …WHAT?" and several other words.

I said, "Can we do this exchange right now, please. You take Ned, and I'll take Vivie back to my cottage. I'll try to stop the friar calling on you until tomorrow, but if he does, please remember your name is Bernard of … no, it's Bernard de Tewkesbury. At least it will be from now on. I am Reginald of Ely. Have you got that?

"Jon is fetching a friar now and a pair of Vivie's shoes. We must have credibility and look as though we are in control of this situation. We need it for them to believe we are serious. They have small donations all the time, but I am going to tell him we are setting up an official Fund for her and whoever else is in that house, with part of it assisting the friars too, of course. That should help persuade them.

"I can afford it now. She is very ill, Bernie. I would judge she needs her drug or whatever it is, urgently, so he must take her back. We can make up the rest of what we should say tonight can't we, and visit them in the morning? Jon will look after Ned.

"They don't know about her fine travelling cape, and they may take it away, doubting it is hers. I'll swear as to its ownership if necessary. They are NOT going to take that cape away from her, do you understand? Once the friar has taken her back, he may return this evening, of course. I hope not, for we need time to get our story straight."

Bernie came over and hugged me, fair crushing my ribs in the process.

"Who is she? What travelling cape? Reginald of Ely, who else? Will you want me to take off my hat, my friend?"

✝

I took Vivie, with the daisies and a slice of honey cake, back to my cottage in the wheelbarrow. I saw a cobweb between two branches on a hawthorn; quick–that will do. Remove the breadcrumbs from the cut first. "Shall I sing you a little song?", she called out. "Isn't this fun?" I just got her inside, still in the wheelbarrow before I remembered her cape was in a heap on the floor. I put my fingers to my lips and said, "Shush. Let's hide it in a cupboard, shall we? One of the good friars should be here very soon. He will give you something to make you feel better and he is bringing a pair of shoes for you to wear so you can go home. Shall I come to see you tomorrow?"

"Oh, I don't think he will let you come. You see, no one is supposed to know about all the people I look after. You won't tell him that Maudie is coming too, will you, because I'm sure he'll be very cross."

Jon appeared as I was speaking, with an anxious-looking young man in tow.

"Thank you for coming, Brother…?" "…Martin", supplied Jon, helpfully. "Brother Martin."

More than a nod of the head was called for here. I held out my hand. "Reginald of Ely; I am one half of the partnership that is setting up the Fund. I realise you must take her back now because she is in pain. Would it be convenient to speak tomorrow?"

The poor man wiped his brow on his sleeve. Here I was, knowing something I should not know, but I had mentioned a Fund.

"Good afternoon, Sir. Er, thank you. Would you care to present yourself at the friary tomorrow morning?" I agreed, and quickly went outside to make sure the large stones on the path were kicked aside so he did not stub his sandalled feet. Vivie was still in the wheelbarrow, daisies in her lap, clutching her piece of honey cake. I put the shoes on for her and stood back.

"This is very sticky," she said, "I don't think that recipe is quite right. It makes your teeth fall out, you know."

That evening I related to Bernie everything that had been said. Jon would be back here, early. We sat and looked at each other. We decided we should find out as much as they would tell us, but the offer of a Fund could smooth the path. Then we mused on whether Bernard de Tewkesbury should first consult the friars about how we should set up the Fund, while I worked out what to do about the cape.

In the morning, armed only with the idea of the existence of the Fund to be established, we decided that all this should be done properly. Either they would trust us, or they would not.

The news on Vivie was as bad as I had feared. When I asked if I could see Mistress Avice, they were not unkind, but she had been missing for two days this time, without any medication, so she had had an extra strong dose.

In the end, they decided we were both worthy citizens who could be trusted. They had indeed been looking after her and "others like her" in that house for several years, but as some of them may otherwise have had antagonistic visitors, only those involved and sworn to silence knew about it. They were free to come and go of course, but often chose not to. All had promised secrecy.

Mistress Avice, they went on to confirm, was very ill indeed. She had never been out overnight before. She was now heavily sedated and probably would not recover, unfortunately. Naturally, they would provide a shroud for her burial. Several of the women who had appreciated her over the years may want her to have a coffin, but that was not necessary, he said, nodding. A shroud would be perfectly acceptable.

Bernard de Tewkesbury then said, firmly and with authority, that for his part he had a store of fair white birchwood which he would provide. He would make her coffin himself.

"Let those women pay whatever they collect, however little it is; give them some dignity too. We will put all that money in the Fund.

"Furthermore," said de Tewkesbury, "We have a travelling cape which is specifically hers." Had he revealed too much? I was watching the tired but not unfriendly face of the elder of the two friars, so I decided to tell them the whole story.

✝

Vivie was buried in a fine white birch coffin, in her travelling cape. We were not allowed to go of course, but the contributors to her coffin went, and we were told she was mourned by more people than she could possibly have imagined. The friars had decided that as Vivie had died, they would move the other women elsewhere as too many people now knew about her house. We thought this was a good decision. It didn't make any difference to our support for the Fund, but we are not part of the new place, wherever it is.

Ned's deft fingers wove me a garland from the last of the Michaelmas daisies, which I fashioned into some sort of circlet. Bernie took Ned back to his cottage to play with his models on the afternoon of the funeral, while I took the circlet up to Vivie's derelict cottage and put it on the stool and said a prayer for Maudie. This was the nearest either of them would come to justice in this world, but Our Lord would surely be forgiving, and more gracious.

I went home and knelt by my bed. I rested my weary head on my arms and cried into the covers. My beard had been a frivolous disguise weighing so light against the nobility of his, and now Vivie's, travelling cape. All my stupid pride over the years, put in the balance against everything those two poor women had suffered: the gulf was immense. And justice?

I came near to despair that evening, until I heard Jeffrey say: "That's how things are. Now get working on it."

"Yes Jeffrey," I said. Justice is about much more than laws. We all must change; surely our whole society must change. There is no room for despair here.

✝

After this sweep of my chaotic life, and all these travelling days, as the Master put it, and before I wade into what happened next when I had a most unexpected visitor, I would like you to be able to put everyone you are about to meet in their proper context.

Let us take a moment to look at this fine market square where we are standing today. Sometimes I forget how much Salisbury has changed since those early days when I was here. The streets around the square are becoming full of our new (and some of those already reconstructed) timber-framed buildings that we put up here, some better than others, and as always, the richer people occupy their chosen sites as the poorer sort are clustered elsewhere.

In this marketplace, wool is already king. It is brought here from all around the countryside to be sold. We are still a domestic market because we are our own customers, and our little industries serve the local churches. We are making some cloth, and clothes for those who live around here, but just wait until we are well established, then for sure we'll start making cloth out of all that wool and sell it far and wide. That will be very profitable.

The trades tend to group together, so the butchers and the fishmongers have their own rows of market stalls near one of the new deep-water drainage channels, and the bakers' stalls are mostly up on oatmeal row. There are a lot of other trades too, and produce stalls. The old blacksmith cum ironmonger had been a good sort, so I heard, but timber-framers got by without him, of course.

In the market square you have a clear sight line from corner to corner, so nowhere will appear to be too far to walk. Our first bishop, Bishop Richard, made sure we were granted a market charter to give us taxes as favourable as those in Winchester. He wasn't mad, I was wrong, just very enthusiastic. Gradually, planned roads led to Salisbury rather than to Old Sarum or Wilton. That caused a stir! In 1228, as I left, the pope had said Bishop Richard had to go to Durham. The city grieved as much as he did , but the canons were at least allowed to choose one of their own as their next bishop. That was such a relief! We have been so fortunate, so blessed. I can say 'we' because I am part of Salisbury again.

The need in any new town is for larger premises where people can live and work and make and store their goods, so building methods are slowly improving as new joints are invented and tried out. This is what I know about. Whatever size and shape your house, your living space is very likely to be communal with a hall and a central hearth, open to the rafters where the soot hangs if there is no louvre for the smoke to escape, and sometimes even if there is. I do wish people would stop and think about which wood burns well. Extra ground-floor rooms may be added on as necessary, of course. The rectangular burgage plots are quite large, although many are subdivided and rented out. If there is an upper floor of any sort it will almost always be reached by a ladder, or perhaps an outside staircase if you live in The Close (which none of our sort do). In Salisbury, our sawpit and the framing place are beyond the 'banging and crashing' Chequers where you will find all the noisier workshops. The houses in The Close, some of which are still being built today, are a different matter; they are very large and grand and are mostly built of stone. When the bishop said he would like to see some stone at least incorporated in our wooden houses, people just muttered: "Yes, but we don't have your means, you know."

Canon Elias, who had looked after my brother Joseph so well, oversaw the whole project. He was well known and liked in this city, once everyone was used to seeing him rushing from drainage ditch to freshwater channel, covered in mud, waving his parchment or slate around, making sure plans were followed. Apparently, as well as everything else, he knew a thing or two about water, coming from the Fenlands himself. They were right, he certainly did.

We are still in the square, but if you turn to face east for a moment, you can see the commercial streets being built, in a not-quite-straight chequerboard pattern. Some plots remain just pegged out, more of those on the fringes, but not too many, considering.

There is a street that has fullers' racks for you to trip over, and some streets have rivulets of water running through them, let in from the river. The Avon sweeps down the western side of the city, past the bishop's mill, and curls around the Close. It drains into the sea at Christchurch. Two sets of sluice gates installed on the river feed our water channels, which flow with the gradient and are a marvel to all who see them. This determines the shape of the layout, of course. It's a pity we can't keep the water cleaner, but then we do have to live and work here.

In these Chequers, as those streets here are called, the shop-fronts line the outside of the square (or nearly-squares) that four streets make, with their stables and workshops and the middens and herb gardens and the odd pig and hens and whatever else, tucked inside. Fortunately, the tannery is located as far away as possible to the east because of the stench. When pigs are out on the loose, they can be a real problem, churning up the dirt roads.

On the eastern side of the cathedral church, up the long high road from Harnham to Old Sarum, beyond the stretch in the city known as Endless to people from the southern end, are the coopers making their casks. Those people also sell old worn-out barrels, broken up for you to put outside your shop for customers to stand on. You can always persuade young Nobby the carter to bring the wood to you if it's too far to carry it yourself; he likes to breathe in the fumes first before he delivers it.

This is the new city. They think they reached about 3,000 souls ten years ago and we certainly haven't stopped growing. We have even become a little more orderly; what with trying to keep our fresh-water channels as clean as possible and regulating those who come in to set up market stalls and moving the city's 'working girls' discreetly out from the centre nearer to Love Lane. Most of them went, so I understand, but officials, counting on their slates, claimed that at least some of them must have retired or gone elsewhere. Well, yes, they had—I knew that now.

I am a curious sort of chap. Here and now in 1260, if you were able to ask a question of the people you meet, you could ask what they remember most clearly from the olden days. Equally as interesting as their answers, would be when they think those olden days were. Little is of interest to us in the world beyond Salisbury, although we are never surprised to be told we are fighting the French and that the king needs our money, so some things filter through, but news usually is what happens in the next street or village or town, so their answers will probably be very local.

Your respondents may well base their thoughts upon the miserable change in the weather; if this is the case, those olden days would be before that. I doubt they would count living up at Old Sarum as the olden days, for that is a world away now.

"The olden days?" they may say, "Wasn't all that before the time there was all the upset when a lot of new people came here from Yorkshire, after Canon Elias and then the bishop died? The second bishop, not the first one. That was before the mid-century, wasn't it? Canon Elias took a great interest in it all, you know. One day someone saw him teaching a group of workmen how to use their pointed spades properly when digging a deep drainage channel. He had such an engaging smile." They had also heard he had told people that he had our cathedral church drawn up in his head even before he came here. Not what you would expect of the clergy really.

Hard-bitten merchants may say everything changed when the southern bridge was built, and the roads all came to Salisbury rather than to Old Sarum or to Wilton. "That's when we knew what growth was all about. They weren't half upset in Wilton."

And one or two grey beards will tell you about the day Archbishop Stephen came to consecrate the first chapels to be built: "That was only about five years into the building work, wasn't it? He was a great man, wasn't he! We all gathered outside, and he spoke to us in English as if he understood us and made us feel as important as all the lords and the rich and powerful people. He made such an impression we never forgot him, or that day." That is one day I remember too. You could see he really approved of what was going on here.

Some will tell you (too many for you to believe they could all have witnessed the incident themselves) of the time Wally Cooper was cavorting in one of the newly dug street water channels. He only had his shirt on and was shouting about how cold it was. He dropped his keys in the water, so when he bent over to hunt for them his shirt rode up and everyone had quite a view. A lot of them bent down to get a better look. Poor Wally. Sometimes he was known as Walt-AAH, as we mimic his wife calling him to heel. I shall always remember Wally. He tried to roll himself in a barrel down Milford Hill once. I didn't see him drop his keys though.

But most often mentioned and missed is Mistress Annie Baker and her famous and most delicious plum bread. It was always sold in the market and before her husband died, from their shop and from a booth up Harnham way as well. "Dear Annie, she was always there for everyone, wasn't she? Even at the end of her life in those darker days, the cold and the rain never stopped her helping people, did it? God bless you, Annie." It was Mistress Annie Baker who became Canon Elias' housekeeper not long before I left, and who had looked after Joseph. Bernie bought one of those plum loaves once when he was queueing up for her tooth powder. I wish I had known how precious it was before the three of us had immediately devoured it.

May God bless us all. Life is hard and often short. We love our city with its many trades and peoples, its pungent smells and hustle and bustle, the clatter of wheels, and the comfort of neighbours, of dogs barking and our individual voices. I am proud to count myself as one of them.

If you are one of us, then you are used to the ordure here, but if you are a little delicate and without a large bunch of thyme to breathe in deeply, then it may knock you flat.

In the evenings, the din and the choking market smells are replaced with woodsmoke escaping from a hundred fires or more, whichever way you face, and stars infinite in the dark sky. Up by the sawpit and along the ridges of the banging and crashing Chequers, there is silence too. The bell for Compline rings out clear, filling the hollows of the night while summoning the angels to keep their watch and guard our sleeping.

You may be wondering why I haven't yet spoken about what is really important. For now, my cathedral church is the huge starry firmament, where Bernie and I come outside to look for our guardian angels each night when we hear the Compline bell. Ned often comes with me, but I don't really know if he understands all I am saying, although he will point up there sometimes. One day, it may be different. Ned may walk without help and I may hold my head up high and not be afraid of my own being. I do miss his mother most dreadfully, and I could never think of seeking to replace her.

Part Four
THE CITIZENS

After Vivie and the friars had brought me to my senses, I suppose I had imagined that we would continue to live our lives in much the same way as before. Bernie still made most of the visits to the market because he is better at shopping, but I did go sometimes, always in my own floppy hat, when he was needed in the sawpit. I remember wondering when Mabel would next be visiting because I was anxious to lay out a herb garden and to learn about their various uses.

Then one morning there was a knock on the door. I called out, "Please come in", as I was bathing Ned's face at the time. A chit of a girl stood there, and then she strode over to where we were. "Let me see," she said as she knelt beside Ned. "Do you have another cushion? He will be a little more comfortable with one on the right-hand side as well." She looked at me and said, "You are the gentleman writing the story of your life, aren't you? Bernie from the pit told me. He said that you wouldn't mind if I came here."

She knelt down by the low daybed and looked Ned over very carefully while she smiled at him all the time. "I see you look after your boy well, Mister Woodman." Where had I heard that before? "That old scar on his head has healed as if someone who knew what they were doing treated it. You will be a woodturner, too, I presume? Can you make some little wooden bowls we can colour?"

She had such authority, I forgot how young she was. I said, "Yes, that's what Mistress Elfrida said." The chit just stared at me before she stood up and then sat down on the bench, hard. "Tell me please–how did you come to know Elfrida?"

I explained that I had met her in Exeter, not long after Ned had been injured, when she had delivered a small Jewish boy to his uncle. She was looking at Ned, then biting her bottom lip as she breathed in very deeply.

Her subsequent smile was warm and heartfelt. "I can help you too," she said. "That lady bequeathed me her life's work. This is what I do." She looked around. "You have a lovely home here, Mister Woodman. May I come to see Ned again? I think I can help you both." Angels don't often turn up in human form, not with freckles anyway. Willing to help me with Ned? I couldn't help being a little curious: "You are surely not old enough to have known Mistress Elfrida?"

The girl was running her fingers along the red groove on the board as she spoke again. "Did you know," she said, "that Mistress Elfrida was the Master's sister?" I must have been shaking my head as I said, "Well, that explains why she had travelled to Exeter from Salisbury then. She really was a remarkable old woman."

Standing up and brushing herself down, the chit indicated my front door: "Outside, I have left you a simple wrought-iron frame and fixings that Ralph, my soon-to-be brother-in-law, has made. It is for a kind of wheelbarrow-cart that has a sloping high back to lean against, and a brake. It is very simple. You could easily make it in wood, he says. He has drawn up his idea for you, here." She handed me the small slate she had in her bag. "There will be a good handle to push, and my sister and Ellie Gardener have devised a thick woollen pad to put in it so Ned and Nobbut will be seated comfortably, and Ned can rest his head too. Ellie is making it now. Bernie said there must be room for Nobbut as well, as he is sure some of the time he would like to ride with his master."

"How well do you know Bernie?" I asked. She replied that she and many of her friends knew Bernie because he was one of those people who helped to fund the winter relief effort each year now the weather seemed to have taken a permanent turn for the worse. "My family and Rob and Ellie and Toby Gardener cook and mend hovels and refurbish clothes. Millie Miller gives us flour, and Tibbsy's nephew gives us milk and as many eggs as he can spare in the winter. I don't know his name, as everyone calls him Tibbsy's nephew, but it is probably Thibault like most of his family. The friars are in charge, of course.``

"Ah, the good friars," I said, "I wonder why Bernie didn't tell me?" I had this strange idea that we were engaged in some sort of swordplay now, and that she was going to win.

"Bernie says you are something of a recluse, but that many people come to the framing place because you give all your knowledge and so much help without any charge, while at the same time you care for Ned so well. And it seems you know the good friars too…" I wondered fleetingly if I should have mentioned that I knew the friars.

She poured some water that was bubbling over the fire into a jug to cool and then went to the hooks where I hung my mint. "Mint," she said, steeping a large handful in the jug. "A refreshing drink and good for you." I didn't like to tell her we often drank it.

Then she wanted to know about the work I had done in Exeter, so I told her. I told her about Jeffrey and Ned's mother too, as well as the Jews who had helped me. I never mentioned I had been here as a young man, of course, but I did tell her how I had come upon Bernie in his hat in the sawpit, so fortuitously. She nodded, "I haven't ever been over to the sawpit before, but I'm sure my sister has, and my friend Toby."

"Your sister looks like you," I said. "I've been here a long time now. I invested in it when I came. Bernie, who owned it all then, was short of capital, you see. With a lot of people wanting timber frames here, it stands to reason it would be a good business." Why was I telling her things I had never told anyone else?

"Tell me about Ned," she said, "What happened?" I forgot how young she was, and I told her everything. She looked at me: "I'm so glad people were kind to you. There is a law about such crimes now, did you know? I understand that the law says that all free men have a right to justice and that justice will not be sold or be denied or delayed."

"Is there? But who could enforce it against the king's men?" She hit her fist, hard, on Jeffrey's board. "One day things will change." She sounded so convinced, so sure, I could almost believe her. What an extraordinary girl.

"May I come on Monday? I am so amazed that you met Mistress Elfrida, and purely by chance it seems."

I replied rather wistfully that I had often wished I could see her again, even if just for an hour, because she had so much knowledge, as well as common sense. "Please come on Monday," I said, "I shall either be here or at the framing place."

"Do you talk a lot to Ned, Mister Woodman?"

"That I do", I said, "I play this little flute and I sing to him too." I picked my flute out of the basket where I kept it.

"Oh, good," she said, "You don't come from around here, do you? What are your songs about?"

"Different things, I suppose," I replied, such as, "when the sea rises up and takes the field floor again." I played a few notes for her.

"Yes, I do see," was all she said in reply. It was then that I realised I didn't know why she had wanted to come here in the first place. I opened my mouth, but she anticipated the question.

"Bernie saw me in the market place and asked me if I would come. Bernie is such a lovely man. It was he who told me about Ned, too. I had a word with Ralph, who is always devising new ideas, hence your barrow-cart.

"Bernie says you have the beginnings of an ulcer on your leg that you are ignoring, when you are not scratching at it, that is. Right, now we'll take off that foul-looking bandage, shall we? Put your leg up on this stool please." What could I say? I had a real sense that I had not been in control of anything since breakfast.

When she had finished, and my leg was tightly bound with a clean bandage, she said, "I must go to see my father now. If I am to come here, please let us not be this formal. My name is Cecily Clerk. People call me Ceci. What is your name Mister Woodman? You weren't baptised Woody Woodman, were you?" Before I could stop myself, I told her.

Nonchalantly, she said, "Reginald, Ned and Nobbut. And Bernie. I shall call on Monday then." She smiled again at Ned, who held out both his hands to her, although I thought he had been dozing in the sunshine. Nobbut left Ned's side so he could go to the door with her. She patted his head and fondled his ears, which is what he had been waiting for. I watched her walk back down the track. Somehow, I knew that our lives were about to change forever.

†

The conversation I had with Cecily Clerk stayed with me from the time she left here on Friday, until the following Monday morning. I had wondered if there was something else that she had wanted to say to me, but I could have been wrong. Bernie had been very bright and cheerful when he arrived home with the shopping because Mistress Tubby had graciously commented on our immaculately presented laundry, so he was wondering whether he dared to slip in his oldest work shirt as well. And Mabel would be coming soon, as she always did, in what he hoped would be a fine mid-summer.

I was wrestling with the sheets that morning, trying to fold them edge to edge in the way Bernie insisted I should before he grovelled his way up Mistress Tubby's street to her most illustrious front door. Oh Bernie, mate! Does anyone else do this, do you think? There was a knock on our door; I knew it wasn't Bernie, he doesn't knock any more. A voice said, "Hello, may I come in?"

I could hear Ned laughing and saying, "Thank you". And there she was, grappling with a lovely thick, full length woollen pad for Ned's barrow-cart.

"I thought if I brought this sooner rather than later," she said, "then you would know the exact size to cut the wood for the barrow-cart so it will fit properly."

She looked at the odd bits of me that were still showing: "What are you doing with those sheets? Here, let me take the long side and you take the other edge." I explained about Bernie's misplaced humility when faced with Mistress Tubby's formidable reputation, and she sighed and merely said, "Why don't we bundle them up like everyone else does and let her earn the fortune she charges!"

Isn't it odd when you feel you already know someone really well when you have only met them once before? "Yes," I said, "I dislike them anyway because they still scratch, and I shall buy some new ones." She told me not to do that until I had met Ellie Gardener. I nodded, not even knowing who Ellie Gardener was. "And your old sheets could probably be returned to you as a wood-working apron or as washing cloths, or food coverings." she said.

She picked her bag up from the floor and took out a package. "I have brought this for Ned to try. Dada used to make us these puzzles. They are quite fun to do. He would draw and colour a picture on a piece of thin wood panelling. Then he would cut it all up into various shapes and jumble them up. You must make the whole picture again. It isn't always as easy as it looks because you can have birds in the air or in trees or on the ground, or when you think you have found someone's leg, it just may belong to someone else. I have drawn and painted Nobbut playing in the trees in your garden, chasing a squirrel." She tossed the pieces in a heap on the board and said to Ned that the only help he would have would be finding the straight edges first. Ned gave a whoop of delight as Cecily led me outside.

The rebel holding the sheets, and the playful girl talking to Ned, changed once again: "I have been thinking about this ever since we met," she said, as we sat on the bench. "I believe I have a problem to solve that may turn either into a wonderful opportunity, or else into a disaster. I am not yet sure which is more likely. I had begun to tell my father who, two years ago in Saint Edmundsbury, had read the personal letters that the Master sent to Joseph each Christmas, which contained a lot of information on what happened at the end of King John's reign, but he was too tired to concentrate after our mid-day meal yesterday, so I had to stop asking him questions." She took a deep breath and said, "I need someone else's opinion before Wednesday. Have you heard of Magna Carta?"

I had no idea what to say. "Well, yes, I suppose I have, but not in any detail. I told you about what happened to Ned: I know that that was so wrong, but what could I have done? Why do you need to know before Wednesday?"

In a few words she told me about a well-dressed, pleasant man coming into the ironmonger's to collect a parcel at least every other week, when she was serving there on Wednesdays. He did not come last week. He had opened the first parcel to check it had survived the journey, and she had seen it was a psaltery with a false back, containing a letter. To cut a long story short, he had noticed she could read and write. He was looking for a scribe, he said, and would he be allowed to explain this to her father? "I am almost certain he is connected to the rebel, de Montfort. Or is de Montfort the king's friend now? I'll have to ask the silk merchant again. Of equal importance is where these psalteries originate."

Suddenly, I wanted to tell her about Vivie, and how there was no justice for her at all. I had heard only de Montfort's name from somewhere I couldn't remember. But if I told her about Vivie, I would have to tell her about the Master and the travelling cape. I looked at her, and she looked at me.

"Reggie," she said, "please stop me if I am wrong, but I think you are Joseph's brother, aren't you? I believe you were here at the beginning, with him. And that you came back here all those years ago, but didn't want to show your face. A new trade? I know that Reginald left for Exeter about a year after Joseph had his accident and was never heard of again. Those dates are right for Elfrida, and what happened to Ned in Exeter. When you played that snatch of a song for me, the one that you often sing for Ned, well that is one of the songs dada used to sing for us when we were children. A true Fenlander's song. And the other day, I slipped in a reference to the Master, and you knew exactly who I was talking about–you wouldn't have done unless you had known him. And your eyes are like Joseph's and your chin is the same shape as his.

"Don't say anything if you don't want to, and I promise that I won't breathe a word to anyone if you tell me I should not, but I also think I am on the verge of a discovery about the part the Master played right at the beginning, before Salisbury was even born, and why Magna Carta is so very important. Also, when I asked the courier who brings them every week, he told me that those psalteries are made in Thetford. Thetford is where Joseph's friend Will's nephew lives. He makes psalteries, it said so in the documents my father and Joseph edited two years ago. I am a little worried that neither Will nor Joseph knows about his part in this."

I stared ahead into the trees, and so did she. "Ceci," I said, "I want you to know about Vivie." I proceeded to tell her everything, which was as painful as when I had first written it down.

Then we sat in silence until I said, "Of course I will help you, if I can."

"Justice." She paused. "Justice. One day. Please, would you meet my father and mother and Rob and Ellie at least? You will find them interesting for what you are writing because, of course, they are first generation people here, with very different backgrounds. And both mother and Ellie were widows. Being a widow is the only way women ever have any independence, you know. All this makes us the people we are. I'll bring them very soon. If you ask them about each other, not about themselves, you could learn much more that way. If you like, I'll ask Ellie to look for some of the finest quality old, second-hand linen sheets for you in the marketplace. She wouldn't ever have anything else. And she will darn any holes, of course."

"Finished!" called a triumphant voice from inside.

Ceci stood up, gave a little bow, and left the bench. "Ah," she said, "I nearly forgot. I wrote out for you the conversation I had with dada yesterday. I expect I put what I felt, so you could leave that out if you like? Here you are. May we all come soon please? I am sure it is time you knew us all. Oh, and I haven't told dada yet that I found Mistress Elfrida's life's work, which she must have hidden in the oak chest in our hall. She knew she was dying when she left Salisbury, you see, and she needed to leave her treasure in a safe place."

It wasn't quite the Monday morning I had anticipated.

Ceci obviously had thought I would agree to writing up her conversation with her father, as if I had been listening to it. And I didn't mind doing it all, as it gives me a better insight. I can see, for instance, that I am not the only person she can twist around her little finger! I must say those letters Joseph has are intriguing. Ceci believes they contain a great deal of information, not generally known, all linked to Magna Carta and, by association, to the 'well-dressed man'. We shall see.

Meanwhile, I am to meet Eustace and Meg and Rob and Ellie and Toby, who will talk about each other. I wonder if this is an occasion for our best clothes and yet another try at making a honey cake that doesn't end up dripping halfway up your arm? But first, based on my notes, here is what happened between Ceci and her father yesterday:

It is Sunday and Eustace is dozing in front of the fire, propped up on a back stool with a cushion behind his neck. He has enjoyed a good and filling mid-day meal, a rare treat in these hungry days when porridge, a little bread and cheese, then one good dish after work was more than most managed. He is vaguely aware that his younger daughter is still at the board, labouring over something or spring can be as hard as winter because your stores are usually running very low. As so often is the case, he doesn't know how his wife does it.

"Dada, who am I?"

Opening one eye, Eustace sees that this is no philosophical question. The girl has her own quill and his ink pot. She is writing. He takes a deep breath, "Do you mean your name?"

"Yes, dada".

He considers for a moment: "Well, I am the Assistant Clerk of the Works, so I suppose you are Cecily Clerk."

"Yes, I thought I probably was. Is that with an 'e' at the end as well as in the middle?"

"It doesn't really matter. As Joseph would have said, do you want them to pronounce it in the old way, emphasising the 'k' with an 'e' after it, or in the newer fashion of swallowing the 'k'?"

Sighing, he was more awake. "Just a moment Ceci, what are you doing?"

"I'm applying for employment, dada."

He was wide awake now, horrified at what he had heard. "You can't do that. You are not a scullery maid. Young women don't apply for work. They don't have work like boys who become apprentices. Why do you keep asking me not to look for a husband for you?"

She looked at him. "I don't want one yet, thank you. But I am nearly one and twenty. Soon Lizzie will be marrying Ralph, now he is a full-fledged blacksmith. Ralph will be in charge at the forge and Lizzie will manage the business. As grandmother has now died, as well as grandfather, you don't need me to help look after her anymore, do you? I can still serve in the shop when it is necessary.

"In fact, a polite, agreeable man has been coming in there, every other Wednesday. Recently, He saw that I could write and, what is more, read back to him all that I had written. He confessed that he could not read or write himself, and said he wanted someone to write letters for him. I told him you were a very respectable man as you worked for the cathedral church, and that you had taught me as well as if I had been a boy. He said he would wish to call on you if you agreed, and if I wrote down a little about myself, he could show it to whoever he works for."

Eustace started to protest, but she continued.

"I was going to say no, but what he said was interesting. He comes in to collect packages that are brought to our ironmonger's shop, for him to take to someone else. The first time it happened he unwrapped the package to see if it had survived the journey. It was a psaltery. He looked at the back and carefully slid the wood aside and I thought I could see a letter in there. Now one comes for him every other week."

Eustace got up and came over to the board: "Psalteries with false backs? Where do they come from? What are you thinking of?"

"That is important, dada. I asked the courier who brought them. They come from Thetford in Norfolk. Now that sounds like Joseph's friend Will's nephew, doesn't it? He lives in Thetford and makes psalteries; it said so in Joseph's own testimony on the founding of Salisbury, in the documents that you both put together. What a coincidence that is. The times you have said how much you would like to write to Joseph, but of course there is no way of getting a letter to Saint Edmundsbury, is there? It has been well over a year now since you spoke to him. You can't ask the canon chancellor again as he wouldn't normally have any reason to communicate with an abbey, would he?"

Eustace realised he could feel the effects of the cup or two of ale he had consumed earlier. He did however have the wit to ask the next question: "And where are these psalteries and letters going?"

Ceci surveyed her father, deciding to deflect the question until she had gathered her own thoughts.

"They are going to someone called Gilbert in Gloucestershire–a Lord, I think, dada. Please tell me again what happened when you took Joseph home, after you had finished editing those reminiscences together, just as Canon Elias had arranged before he died. It was such a good story. And then what happened when Joseph brought out those personal letters Canon Elias had written to him. That was when he told you what was in them..."

Eustace settled down again. "Why are you so interested in the Master's letters? I still think of him as the Master, I can't help it."

"Because he was Lady Elfrida's brother," she replied. His head was still not quite clear enough to see the connection, but no matter.

He began, as always when he told this story, with its back story, even if it was unnecessary. He reminded her that Joseph had been the apprentice mason who, having fallen from the scaffolding, had been taught by the Master while he was recovering, learning to read and write in Latin and in English. It was fertile ground and they had discussed the Scriptures at length before he sponsored the boy through the new schools in Cambridge, close to his boyhood home near Ely. They had always kept in touch, writing annually throughout Joseph's eventual career as a schoolmaster in Saint Edmundsbury, right up until the time the Master died.

Joseph had kept all thirteen of those treasured long and personal letters. He had never previously met Eustace, having left for Cambridge before Eustace's arrival, but he did indeed come to Salisbury for the consecration as he had been instructed.

This was easy; Eustace loved remembering the details. He told her again how the canon chancellor had accompanied them to Saint Edmundsbury after the Christmas of 1258, their editing of a story about the founding of Salisbury done. What a dreadful winter it had been, but the clergy had many contacts along the route, so they had stayed quite comfortably in manors owned by the Church.

"The abbey was vast–vast is a good word, Ceci–and so wealthy.

We were greeted very civilly, and after supper we all slept in pilgrims' cells that first night, as we had arrived so late. Then the next morning Joseph was due to teach his class straight after breakfast, so the canon chancellor and I went along too.

"When we all arrived at the school, his class was sitting quietly with the prior. Evidently, they had not been told their magister was returning that day. The whoops of joy when he appeared, and their faces, well! Young Scoulding rushed to a cupboard and pulled out a decidedly lopsided low stool he had just made and carefully placed it under Joseph's lame foot, while he leant on his desk and sat down. It didn't end there, either. Joseph spent the day telling them all about us, and those children kept looking at us all in amazement. Only Jackson major broke the spell when he couldn't contain himself any longer. He turned to the canon chancellor and said, 'I beg your pardon Sir, but do you really have water running in little rivulets through your streets? Gosh!'

"After lessons we were all dragged to his home by the children, to a feast and more presents. The boys' parents had been secretly forewarned so, using the key he had left with his colleague Will, they had spent the day cleaning and decorating Joseph's cottage with holly and candles, then lit a fire and laid out the food they had made. Widow Pryke had sewn him some new bed linen and I thought she looked as though she would happily share it with him. She stuck to him like fish glue, although he didn't notice, and he was overwhelmed anyway by everything else. At the school that day, Will hadn't said a word about any of it, so he just beamed all evening like some little cherub who had kept a big secret.

"Those pupils loved our Joseph, Ceci. He only had to raise an eyebrow for total silence to fall. I had forgotten, but he had more meagre eyebrows when he arrived home because our barber here, where I had taken him after he had been more than a month on the road, had set to and trimmed off fifty years' worth of growth with the determination of a man clearing a thorn thicket."

"Now please tell me about the Master's letters to Joseph," said his relentless interrogator. "The things you did say were so interesting; it showed the Master in a completely different light. Can you remember more than that?"

"Joseph showed them to me one evening before I came back home with the canon chancellor. They were so detailed, as if the Master was trying to remember for himself as much as for Joseph."

Eustace, feeling full and content, liked to reminisce. "I haven't quite got your memory, Ceci, nor dear Annie Baker's, for the words that were spoken or written, so here it is as I remember it. Don't forget that questions asked in one letter weren't answered until the next year but piecing it all together was fascinating.

"Joseph, far from Salisbury and perhaps nostalgic for his old life, was interested in what had happened before any of them had arrived there, and he had asked the Master many questions.

"The answers were all such a surprise. Perhaps it was easier for the Master to speak of those things remotely, when he felt he could not say very much at all to his friends and colleagues, some of whom may have been involved in the drama one way or another.

"As all this happened before the founding of our city, Joseph had not thought any of it was relevant to the story we were editing between us."

Still trying to coax him along to a starting point, Ceci encouraged him further: "I shall close my eyes, dada, and you can talk to me as if it is happening now."

"Ah Ceci, not now–when I'm fully awake, I promise."

He sat down and closed his eyes again. His daughter looked at him, a little disappointed, and thought her own thoughts by the fire.

Then he started quite suddenly and looked around. "How many bells did I just hear? Meg will be having an afternoon nap. Where is Lizzie? She must be with Ralph. How did it become as late as this?"

"How indeed, dada! Another time soon, then." She ruffled his thatched head affectionately and left the hall, running her fingers along the edge of the lid of the oak chest as she did so.

✝

My little brother! I read what Ceci had written again and again, trying to get to know him. Perhaps she had even asked her father for these details, just for my sake?

On Saturday afternoon (that young woman doesn't waste any time), Ceci reappeared, this time with her parents, and with Rob and Ellie as well as their son, Toby. I did know they were coming because Ceci had met Bernie at the Tuesday market, passing by as she and Ellie were examining the linen on the second-hand stall.

Of course, I had told Bernie about all that had happened, and he very much approved. He did also say that he could not possibly face Mistress Tubby with sheets in the state Ceci and I had left them on my hall floor, and please could I fold them up? Bernie also said, quite firmly, that he and Ned would play with his models–with only one jug of water–on Saturday afternoon, so we would not be disturbed if I was attempting to write things down. He is still of the opinion there is something magical about forming letters, a rite into which he has not been initiated, however often I ask him if he would like to try.

"Furthermore," said Bernie the next day, "if you make a honey cake, Ned and I will take it to my cottage, out of your reach. It's less messy that way. I have ordered a dozen small, griddle breads for you from Old Jeb, who makes a fine griddle bread, even if his rye bread is a bit hard for my gums now. I'll collect them on Saturday morning, and you could toast them and serve them with butter? And perhaps you could put some of that lavender from your garden into the finger bowls?"

Oh, Bernie. I couldn't help thinking that no-one had ever looked after me anywhere near as well as Bernie does now, even when I was a child. I think he needs Mabel to care for, so getting her here, and keeping her here, must be in my next great plan.

I did put on my best clothes on Saturday, but I needn't have bothered. What lovely people they are. My little hall was full of chatter and laughter. The breads were just right, and Ellie brought me the sheets she had found and mended. Toby, looking exactly like his father, had showered me with questions. Eustace had already written down his thoughts for his and Meg's contributions, and Ceci took her father and mother out to see my garden while Toby explained the note he had written for me about himself and his parents. I was overwhelmed.

These people were my friends now; how wonderful that sounded. I just collected everything together, and said I would work on it very soon, and would they like to meet Ned? Of course, they would. We went down to Bernie's. They departed soon afterwards, having had to leave Lizzie to mind the shop. "She doesn't want to write anything yet. You will see why later," said Eustace, meaningfully.

✝

Eustace is the assistant Clerk of the Works at the cathedral church and is judged almost a newcomer. I say almost, because he was here before the weather changed for the worse and the Master died; these are still two of the definitive time markers in Salisbury. He was brought here by the Master only in 1235, being also the man he chose to co-edit the manuscripts collected by them both about the founding years of the new city.

Eustace helps to manage the stonemasons' yard, do the ordering, and produce the accounts. He is still the deputy in charge of transport and deliveries and a host of other things. He married Meg, the widowed daughter from the ironmonger's in Salisbury, just off the Market Square—"up Endless", as it is called by those who come up this long High Street from Harnham, south of the new city. Eustace and Meg now live in a house between the Market Square and The Close, and have two daughters, Elizabeth and Cecily, known to all their friends as Lizzie and Ceci. Apart from their appearance, Meg and Lizzie, the elder daughter, are very alike in temperament; and as he says: "strong-willed, pert, astute, and appealing," And happily for him dealing with such bundles of energy, very predictable.

Many years before, a senior churchman called Elias (he wasn't then quite yet our Canon Elias) had offered to employ one of the boys from a trusted family known to him from his own village in the Norfolk Fen country. Consequently, it was at that time young Eustace was sent to Canterbury, seemingly just as a servant, while Elias was in exile in France (again), but we'll come back to that. The nature of the job was explained to him; watching the archbishop's back, to put none too fine a point on it. The boy understood that discretion was everything.

When the archbishop died ten years later in 1228, Eustace was then asked to go to Durham with similar instructions, to help Bishop Richard, who had just very reluctantly moved there from Salisbury at the lord pope's command, to sort out some of their grim problems. Elias had become our Canon Elias well before then, in 1220, and he made sure Eustace was taught to read and write while he was in Durham. Eustace has had an unusual career, to say the least, and it didn't stop there.

Canon Elias died in 1245, but he had said that Eustace was to await a visit at the time of the consecration from someone as yet unknown to him. The visitor and Eustace would, the Master had believed, make very good joint editors of the documentary work then still in progress, on the founding of the new city. The unknown person would turn out to be my brother Joseph, now a schoolmaster, but once an apprentice stonemason like me.

✝

Meg, Eustace's devoted little wife, still looks exotic with her olive skin and large brown eyes and indescribably unruly, corkscrew hair. There is no other way of describing it that I can think of.

Her father had been affectionately known by the whole of Salisbury's hard-working make-do-and-mend fraternity as "Smiffy". Smiffy was a good craftsman, jovial, helpful and didn't overcharge you. At the forge he trained his apprentices well. Those apprentices often had sisters who started out as servants to Mistress Smith, but they were never happy in her employ as she was much more demanding even though she only had one child (it had been a complicated birth, as she would tell you): their daughter, Meg.

Those girls all tended to leave quite quickly for one reason or another, so as Meg was growing up she learned to cope well on her own, while her mother, with all her infirmities, pondered on her lack of inclination for being a blacksmith's wife, or for even serving behind the counter in their ironmonger's shop. In her head those infirmities grew ever more dire. None of this prevented her from telling people how wonderful "her Eddie" was because she must have known she tried the patience of her even-tempered husband to the limit.

Meg would have liked some company of her own age, and she did sometimes worry about herself and her father looking just a little different in some regards to most of the population of Salisbury. Smiffy thought one of his ancestors may have come from some unspecified wild mountains; perhaps even a Moor from southern Spain had pitched up at Old Sarum as a stonemason, working on one of the two earlier cathedrals? It had never worried Smiffy.

A well-turned-out soldier, under the command of the Earl of Cornwall, appeared at the right time and after a brief and formal courtship, had asked her father if he might marry the girl. Smiffy, very fond of his daughter, saw a fine man who could eventually take over the business. Meg told her father she thought she had detected livestock in the man's beard. The livestock vanished overnight, but Meg stayed in her room.

The beard disappeared the second night and, to please her father, Meg was persuaded. But after the ceremony, unfortunately, this soldier turned out to be wholly uninterested and uninvolved in their marriage. All he had wanted was to gain a dowry and a livelihood for when he could no longer go a-soldiering. The beard was immediately re-grown, and he went off very regularly to war, in the boisterous company of his fellows and cronies.

Nothing was said at home, but Smiffy suspected, and was mortified; his lovely girl with no marriage at all. The soldier was killed in France eventually, unmourned at the forge or in the ironmonger's. It was the deceit that rankled. Smiffy was aware his choice had been disastrous, and that Meg must choose a husband for herself. They waited quite a while, but one Sunday in Saint Thomas' church she spotted this interesting-looking newcomer in the aisle across the way, with his striking straw-thatched head. Eustace was introduced to her by Mistress Annie Baker, the Master's housekeeper, who knew everyone.

Meg of course was only too aware of her advancing age, so no time was lost and she produced two daughters in two and a half years. Everyone was exhausted, including Eustace. The neighbours all helped this little family because they knew Eustace worked long hours in the Yard for the Master, whose fame as the eccentric but thoroughly likeable canon from the cathedral church had reached well beyond the confines of The Close.

✝

Throughout her childhood Ceci had the feeling that she was that ripple in the mill pond that came along after the big splash her elder sister had made. She was always a little in awe of her, she says, because she is so funny and vivacious, like their mother. They only had to look at each other to burst out laughing, and that wasn't because dada said he thought her mother's hair looked like an untrimmed yard broom or anything like that. They both had a little flame which sparked and then sparkled when they were in the room. Somehow Lizzie always forgot there were pots and dishes to be cleansed after a meal, though.

They never employed any kitchen help because the maids, when their mother had been a child, had all bolted fairly quickly, so she said. Meg became used to running a kitchen, helping in the shop, looking after the girls, looking after her mother ("I do feel so ill today, Meg") and feeding the apprentices in the forge, and that was before we attempted to feed the five thousand every day in the winter! Lizzie helps to do all this now; she has grown up a lot recently, and she will make someone a marvellous wife. And his name is Ralph. Ceci writes:

"We seem to cook for half of Salisbury each winter because of all the hungry people here now the harvests are bad. Some starve throughout these cold, wet winters we have had of late. It is terrible to see. Their children may not be fed at all if we don't do it. I used to get up early most days and creep outside to the kitchen to make a start. My father always came along to see if there was anything he could do to help before he went down to the Yard.

"I wish a house could have a book. Of course, it can't. You

have to be so rich to own a book, but dada did have a few Latin texts he was made to copy out when he was working for Bishop Richard in Durham. I worked out what it all meant and devoured those while Lizzie and Toby Gardener were having a little rebellion over having to learn any Latin at all. I'm a bit younger than them, so I wasn't included ('So which rebellious baron are we today, young Toby, eh!?') They were funny. Dada used to sigh deeply and hit the front of his head with the flat of his hand sometimes.

"Looking back, I can see there was a remarkable absence of what people call discipline. Dada doesn't believe in hitting girls anyway. I had listened when he and Joseph were discussing it. Joseph said he never had to discipline his class–who are all boys, of course–because showing firmness through kindness and reasoning with them is so much better. I can only remember my mother angrily chasing Lizzie around the kitchen once with a wooden spoon, when she had said something very rude. Maybe we just weren't bad children.

"When Toby came to play, Lizzie always chose the games. Toby was such a well-mannered little boy, he never said anything, but we did share a secret smile sometimes.

"It is difficult when you are a woman as we do not have a voice. It is important to me that I can do something to help people. Dada has had such an interesting life, but that is because he is a man. If he or mother says 'Ce–ci,' to me again in that tone of voice that surely means when will I look for a husband, and if it isn't soon they will look for one for me, I'll scream inside my head. How can I have one of those until I know who I am?

"I have found Lady Elfrida's secret treasure, in our oak chest in the hall. I have, I have! Dear Joseph transcribed it all from her terrible script, so I am reading and learning a little each day. I can't see anyone allowing me to go to visit the Moors in southern Spain as she did, but it is all so marvellous. All her life's medical work, her learning about illnesses and their causes. Some of the herbs she uses for remedies I have never heard of. What can be done for beaten and mistreated women, and for the destitute whom no one visits, not even the good friars. I shall have to tell dada soon, because I need him to do something very important for me. That all confessed, I feel better now."

Poor Ceci! Caged, not because of her parents who are very understanding, but by the society in which we all live. I think from the way she has ended, that she will soon have to again question Eustace about my brother Joseph's cache of letters from the Master. I am becoming very interested in them myself!

✝

Try as I might, I could only dimly remember Rob from the early days, which only means that I hardly ever went to see my brother when he was living at Leaden Hall. I am ashamed of that all over again. I do see what Ceci means when she says that these first people in Salisbury have interesting and varied stories to tell. Ellie is so matter of fact about her life, I can only admire her for it. I have summarised all that they told me about their family:

Just north of the market square, but not far away from Eustace and Meg's house, Ellie is reflecting. She had never known who she really was. She had spent her early childhood with her grandmother, but without being loved, in the nearby town of Wilton. She had few memories, fond or otherwise, of those years.

The nightmares had begun when she was sent to live with the nuns at Wilton Abbey. Everyone knew this was an abbey of great importance, but equally they were also aware of its current serious financial difficulties.

Ellie didn't know why she had no mother, but imagined she died giving birth to her. Grandmother had never said. Her father was also a mystery, his absence a matter for pursed lips. She was left in no doubt that her mother had sinned and that a price had to be paid. Her father, whoever he was, had given the nuns no dowry for her, so her status as a servant was assured. However, she was a servant who was taught to do needlework instead of scrubbing floors, so was he of the middling sort? Perhaps he didn't even know about her.

Such thoughts sustained her through all the years she was there. Those less fortunate servants–those with their hands too often in water too hot or too cold and those with callouses on their knees–what had they done to harm anyone? Ellie tried to show sympathy, but it was met with jealousy and shrugged shoulders and sometimes a sly kick to her ankles.

They weren't all unkind, but one of the nuns knew how to show her disdain. Near perfect sewing was criticised: "Do it again!" accompanied by a sneer and a curled lip. Any of them would give her a slap if they felt particularly aggrieved, but no one ever hurt her hands.

Grandmother was allowed to come to see her twice a year, but had nothing much to say until once, when she suddenly came out with, "I'm going to get you out of here." Ellie thought about that every day, and then again just after her night-time misery, when she was unable to stop thinking about her lost parents. The nuns said nothing at all, but on the next visit she was told by her grandmother to stop being so useful or the price would go up.

Ellie had noticed some of the girls there, novices who had a dowry, were becoming more spiteful. She was told she was too pretty, and to cover herself up. This had worried her because she was already having trouble evading a particular priest as he slithered around corners to be near her. She did not know it, but the abbess had also realised that the girl was too intelligent for her own good, and more to the point, for their good. Their sewing and mending asset was becoming a liability, and she was suddenly delivered into the hands of her grandmother for a price she never knew.

Grandmother had no wish to keep this manifestation of her daughter's shame in the town. She had already surveyed Wilton's younger sons, those who would not inherit and were therefore freer to marry as they wished, as they hoped to pick up some small dowry in return. The shy girl was manoeuvred to meet Martin Roper, second son of Old Ropewalk, as he was known. "Hard rough hands and a hard rough heart," those in the know said, with these traits already evident in his firstborn.

Martin, the second son, had been overlooked in all regards, but was a much kinder person for it. He only had to gaze upon the golden angel set before him and he was head over heels in love with her. Grandmother had calculated well, and Ellie had at last found someone who cared. They married as soon as possible and some coin had changed hands–but neither of them knew which way it went.

Old Ropewalk had already died when Martin and Ellie began married life in a shop in the Chequers in Salisbury, where they would sell the rope for the family, although never owning the profits; only being given back just enough money to live on. They didn't care because they were free. Martin bought Ellie a piglet to rear, and it lived out the back in the Chequer interior with full access to the midden. Grandmother in Wilton then died, so Ellie knew she could never ask any more questions, nor obtain any answers.

Disaster struck the following year in Salisbury when Martin was hit as a cart overturned on Bridge Street, and he died shortly afterwards. Everyone was so sorry, but it had been no one's fault, just the result of too much wheeled traffic.

Elder brother, the owner of the Rope Walk and the family business, stepped in. He reduced the money paid to Ellie because there was only one mouth to feed instead of two, and told her that she was fortunate because he would still deliver the ropes to her, 'personally'. His leering got him nowhere. In fact, then he had to resort to visiting *That Avice* two doors along and around the corner. The traumatised Ellie covered herself up completely and gave all her attention and affection to Miribel, her pig.

It was at this point that Mistress Baker and her husband moved to the corner plot to open a bakery, and she and Ellie became lifelong friends, with Ellie the grateful recipient of her company and much help, although still eventually Miribel had to go to slaughter because Ellie could not afford to keep her.

A few years later, when they had mourned the death of Annie Baker's little son together, and found more besides that bonded them, Annie became housekeeper to Canon Elias after her husband died. It was a good while before she then realised that Ellie was appearing at her cottage whenever handsome, dark-haired Rob the gardener and handyman came with her weekly gift of vegetables from the Master.

†

The Master had given Rob a job when he saw him begging for work on the building site, long ago in the days when the foundations for the cathedral church were still being laid. Unknown to anyone there, Rob was a runaway serf, ill-treated by his masters, so had been unable to say anything about his background. He was, therefore, as reticent as Ellie was shy, and the whole idea Annie had about his marrying Ellie seemed hopeless–that is until Mistress Elfrida, the Master's sister, paid a visit and she and Annie Baker between them organised a masterstroke.

Elfrida, a trained apothecary along with her many other medical skills, taught Ellie–as her 'practitioner', as she called her–how she could manipulate Rob's shoulders, which had been somehow damaged in childhood. It worked like a dream. He had turned up at Annie's cottage as usual with the Master's gift of produce one Saturday morning, having been told by Mistress Elfrida that she would have a 'practitioner' there, waiting to massage his shoulders. And this was how Rob was able to believe at last that he should set about asking Ellie to marry him–at which point he became one of the happiest men alive.

Years before, he had escaped from his manor with the help of old Tibbsy, a regular visitor there as the purveyor of the best eggs in the district. Tibbsy had a cart and plenty of sacking to hide under, so when Rob's old father died, he was able to help him run away.

Rob, like so many of the children he had known, had no mother he could remember. Nor had his father, a serf, had any means of preventing those in charge at the manor becoming his son's tormentors and roping great blocks of stone to Rob's neck, making him race against other child serfs for their sport. Even now, Rob lived with the fear that they might one day seek him out in The Close and reveal his shameful past, cruelly breaking his years of silence, and drawing from him the history of the deception–which all spelt trouble for the Master. No wonder Rob rarely showed himself in Salisbury.

Summoning up every ounce of the courage he had never previously found, Rob approached the Master and told him his whole life story, and declared that he wished to be married to Ellie.

What happened next entered folklore. On Monday morning, Rob was told to saddle up the Master's favourite horse. The Master, angrier than anyone there had ever seen him (you could tell from his eyes, apparently), paid the tormentors an official visit with the relevant papers he had made sure were drawn up by the bishop's clerks. Rob was immediately set free.

People were quite certain afterwards, when it was said that it would never happen again at that manor, that it was true beyond any doubt. Occasionally, a version of what had been said leaked out, but we should perhaps draw a veil over what may or may not have taken place that day in that God-forsaken hellish pit.

The Master rode back to The Close and found Rob and Ellie standing together under his bent old apple tree, waiting for him. He just put his arms around them both.

Ellie now knew how to massage Rob's neck so he could work without pain. She walked out of the elder brother's shop, leaving a month's rent on the counter, and then after that she and Rob were married, as soon as it could be arranged. Later, she used her sewing skills to great effect for the canons and their households in The Close. The wonder of it all never left either of them.

Ellie could only hope it was not too late for her to have children. With good fortune, in due course, Tobias, her only son, was born in the accommodation where they lived, above the stables at Leaden Hall. When the Master died, they moved to the cottage next door to Annie Baker.

Over time, the two families, Rob and Ellie and Toby, and Eustace and Meg with their two children, both supporting their much-loved honorary grandmother, and together with the good friars, became the focal point for the winter relief effort in the city as the weather deteriorated, year on year.

✝

Eustace couldn't wait to tell me about his failings as a schoolteacher; so unlike my talented brother, he said!

Toby Gardener is nearly a year older than Lizzie Clerk and a little more than two years older than her sister, Ceci. This hardly matters. It was natural that the families should grow closer as the children played together in each other's homes like puppies in a basket.

At the appropriate time, and despite Eustace's best efforts, Toby and Lizzie completely failed to learn any Latin. Perhaps they couldn't think why they should. Eustace realised very early on that Lizzie was probably the ringleader in all this. He smiled to himself; they were predictably alike, his daughter and his wife. He had never been able to persuade Meg that it would be better if the shutters in their bedroom fitted properly, even if it wouldn't be as much fun. Stubborn to the last!

However, Toby and Lizzie were quick, and it became evident that Toby thought deeply about what he was saying. From the beginning they both knew the sounds of the letters of the alphabet and were delighted when they could write their names and read what each other had written. They were encouraged to write short words–whereupon for a while Toby's cat spent most nights asleep with c-a-t written on a slate propped up beside him. They could add and subtract (the even numbers were easier, they decided) and assign one of those numbers to an invoice or to a slate to identify the appropriate customer, whose name they could now read.

They learned how to debate. Joseph had explained to Eustace that he was taught this skill by the Master. Eustace was a little puzzled because it seemed to him the children just became better at arguing with their parents. He was relieved they were such good children, generally. He read them stories he had written for them, and they read them back to him. He did worry that there were not many opportunities to practise writing as the slates they had were rather small.

The day Lizzie wrote 'silver penny' on her slate, Eustace wondered if he was winning. Later however, Lizzie's household budgeting and accounting exercises were spectacular in their inventiveness:

Item: Fysshe half price at stall 2 with my nice smile.
NOT stall 4
Item: Best bred free from Granny Annie
Item: Big meat 560 or 600 silver pennies. Don't like liver. Hate tripe.

At that point, Eustace wisely capitulated. Her mother could teach her more usefully. Toby would practise faithfully all he had learned so far and would not be afraid to ask questions; why, the child was truly eloquent in his praise of Gribble's messy hunting skills and the resultant deliveries on to the rushes in Rob's hall.

Thankfully, Eustace turned his full attention on Ceci, who having worked quietly by herself all along, was by then, he sensed, well beyond just the few Latin texts he himself had known. Teaching, he decided, was not as simple as it was made out to be.

He arranged riding lessons for all the children with young Nobby, the carter. Nobby, son of old Nobby, had been successful in business, employing two other young men. He kept good stables and looked after his horses well. If you lived in the countryside, riding seemed to come naturally; so many things to think of, living in a city.

†

I sat down one afternoon with Ellie and Toby so they could both tell me about Toby's childhood. Each of them certainly seemed to agree with what the other had said. Toby was a dutiful and happy child, at home, performing every task asked of him, so his mother tells me.

Unfortunately, as he followed his father around, Toby himself realised he did not particularly like gardening or repairing houses. He had tried hard, but he disliked hens even more because when he was only six, they had pecked his bottom a lot when he was helping old Mister Tibbsy. He had to bend right down to gather the eggs from their nesting boxes, and then Mister Tibbsy would say that he shouldn't make faces at them. If you didn't want to upset poor old Mr Tibbsy, what would you do if you were a small boy with a hen, who thought you were robbing her nest, pecking at your bottom?

Toby admitted that secretly he had dreamed of a different life, of being a knight in armour and doing good deeds. As a little boy he knew he had earned much goodwill from his running of many errands, so he was thinking of those thin metal rings you can buy from the ironmongers: one dozen in assorted sizes for a fourth of a silver penny. He saw they had many uses. His father had a large one around his thick leather purse and his mother used the tiny ones to secure her linen lavender bags. He thought he could also use one of the middle-sized ones himself, around that pouch where he kept the half-sucked boiled honeyball that Granny Annie made for him without anyone knowing. If he was quiet, he decided he could carefully thread one or two onto Gribble's tail while he was asleep. And if he asked his father to put a hook on the wall he supposed he could hang one on it and thread his leather thongs through it, or just use the hook itself, of course.

They were both laughing as Ellie told me that Sir Toby decided three dozen (assorted) would make a good showing. His father gave him a half of a penny and then another quarter of one. He duly visited the girls' grandfather in his ironmonger's shop and was given a preferential price, three dozen for the price of two. Then he asked his mother if she could use some of his older clothes that still fitted him, and sew the metal rings onto his sleeves and his hose, like chainmail. He offered to return to his father the unspent 'fourthing' but he was told it was his to keep and had received a big hug as well.

Ellie found an old linen shift, as well as Rob's worn-out, black gardening hat, returning them as a tabard with a Gribble Passant Sable motif sewn onto it. Toby said he was so excited. He knew that all knights wore chainmail, but not what sort of helmets they wore these days. You had to be able to see out.

"He consulted Lizzie," said his mother, trying hard to keep a straight face. "That little horror then advised him to beg at the fishmongers' stalls (except for number 4). Someone eventually gave him one of those old deep, slatted square kipper-boxes. The smell was terrible. Rob had smoothed off any rough edges, and when Toby stuck it on his head he found it rested nicely on his shoulders. He had looked out of his new helmet so proudly, between two of those slats. In his armoury was a lance made from a hazel stick. A hazel stick sword with a willow hilt bound on with twine followed, to complete our knight's apparel."

Regretfully in some ways, according to his mother, little boys grow up. About the time he realised he had down on his upper lip, Toby remembered walking home one day carrying a bucket of sawdust from the sawpit.

It was the day after the night he had a vivid dream about a bell. It was a lovely bell, deeply sonorous and round of sound, the sort that made your heart sing. He had gazed upon it in the foundry. The bell-makers had liked the look of him because he was big and strong, but the heat had been unbearable, even standing at a distance. So, for him bells were only for joyous listening. He loved the depth of their many tones, especially as the sounds came rolling towards you through the frosty air.

Toby had awoken with such a start, he wondered if he had been asleep at all, but instead somehow walking up and down in the Chequers. The trouble was he couldn't remember ever seeing the bell foundry up there, but strangely he seemed to have known what a bell foundry looked like. He offered to go to collect some more sawdust from the pit so he could explore the whole Chequer and the streets around. There was nowhere even resembling a bell foundry.

It had just been a dream then, but he found it rather disturbing. What was he seeing? Then he identified the exact place where he thought he had seen the bell, so he could never escape the memory.

At this point in our conversation, Toby sent his mother into the garden. And I have the first glimpse of someone else coming across the "well-dressed man" in the ironmonger's.

Increasingly, Toby said, he felt the weight of both families' expectations that he would wish to marry one of the girls. In truth, he was quite relieved when Lizzie made it clear she would be spoken for by Ralph, an apprentice blacksmith. Instinctively, he had harboured the thought for a while now that possibly she could eat him alive. Ceci was lovely, but had grown too remote and too clever, he thought, for a simple would-be chivalrous knight.

When he reached his majority, with no prospective wife and no occupation he particularly wanted to follow, he had once found a willing girl but consequently spent a long time afterwards worrying about what they had done. Occasionally he walked in the direction of Love Lane, but decided those consequences would be even more worrying, so he always turned back and went straight home.

He remembered his parents saying that in the far-off days up on the hill-fort (you never know it may even have been half a hundred years ago), you had to do your penance in public, not like now. Toby decided not to go to S. Thomas' where both families worshipped, but walked instead down to the new cathedral church. He approached a canon walking along the grass verge. This canon was human and forgiving of someone such as he, so he was glad he was living in these new times.

And one day, quite recently in fact, when he was talking to Ceci who was serving behind the counter in the ironmonger's, the well-dressed man came in (velvet jerkin, embroidered gloves, red leather shoes) to see Ceci. He heard him say that he was looking for someone to ride into Gloucestershire one day each week, as well as hoping to find a scribe. So now Toby has seen the stranger too.

Later, Ceci told him all she knew, which wasn't very much. The man collected a package with a psaltery in it most weeks, and she believed it was to be taken to a knight called Gilbert who was helping someone called Simon de Montfort. He was the one who was trying to persuade the king that his parliaments or councils could include some ordinary people, and he was ready to fight for such a cause, he declared. All this seemed to fit with ideas for government and the law in that great charter, the one that Joseph had said Canon Elias had so treasured, but she wasn't sure how.

Toby said that he believed he had found a Cause. Ceci was more cautious. She said she didn't think it could be quite as simple as that. Her father had been rather alarmed when she told him, so she had not mentioned it to anyone else. Ellie came in from the garden at that point and asked whether we had finished our man-to-man talk?

✝

I couldn't sleep. The more I thought about it, the more sure I was that Ceci had questioned her father in such a way that I could find out about my brother. I wonder if Joseph still thinks about Emma. I'm sure he does because I can see now that Emma must have seemed like a mother to him. I thought of Ned, without a mother, and cried into my pillow. Then I realised how Bernie had so skilfully and unobtrusively stepped into that huge void.

How very considerate Ceci is. I treasure that picture I have of Joseph now, a quiet boy grown so much older and happier and at peace with himself. I was also in no doubt of the part the Master had played in all of this.

What can I do to help Ceci with this stranger that she knows nothing about? I must leave her to talk to her father about the Master's letters, first. I can see they could be so revealing. She returned to see me briefly the other day, asking if she could borrow what I had written so far about my early days here, in case there were any clues there that could help her? It isn't very much, I told her, and passed it to her straight away. She then asked if I knew Millie Miller. I said that I didn't, and she said not to worry as she would somehow find the time to go to see her. A little while ago, there had been some sort of altercation at Fish Stall Number 4 apparently, when someone had been heard to mention the well-dressed man coming out of the ironmonger's. I had heard something about Fish Stall Number 4 before, I think.

The following Tuesday after the midday meal, Eustace went to look for his daughter. She was in the girls' bedchamber, sewing with enormous stitches great bands of sacking to cover the front and the back of the hem of a skirt. On the bed lay something that may have been half a sleeve, sewn in sacking from elbow to wrist.

"Ceci, whatever are you doing?"

"Dada," she said, not looking up until she had reached the join where she had begun. Then she put it down and took a deep breath. "I wanted to speak to you, because you see I have found our treasure. It must have been in your oak chest by the door in the hall all this time.

"The Master's sister, Lady Elfrida, had left it for us, as she trusted you and because she must have known she was dying. Alongside her testimony on her visit to Salisbury, for the story Canon Elias had envisaged, she left all her notes on her life's work in medicine. You wouldn't have looked at it because of her impossibly difficult writing. Joseph laboured over it all for a while before he realised it was not relevant as part of your story, but he finished working on it anyway. He was such a diligent man. He just put it all back in the chest with the other documents. She did not know–because I was not yet born–but you see, somehow she had left it there for me, hadn't she?"

Eustace looked at his daughter for a long while. He wanted to remember her just as she was now, and as she had been as a child.

"Before you tell me any more," he said quietly, "would you like to hear about the Master's letters to Joseph?"

"Yes please, dada." No wheedling was necessary now. As Eustace sat on her clothes chest, he said:

"Firstly, Ceci, you must tell me why you need to know all this. I admit, thinking it through now, I can see that all these things we did not use in our text could still be of some importance. I understand your attraction to Elfrida's work that you found in my oak chest. But what about old King John, and why did the archbishop and Canon Elias go to such lengths to achieve what they did? What is this charter exactly?"

"We are ordinary people, and I don't know either," admitted his daughter. "But I believe now it has recently been proclaimed in English and the Church supports it. If there is a man out there, called Simon de Montfort, who thinks he must defend it with his life, then I do want to know. I don't mind working for an honourable person, writing menial letters at a distance if he is serving this man, but is this dangerous, do you think? Everyone held the Master in such high regard, yet that was because he gave us our cathedral church, and Thomas Becket, his shrine. All those fine talents he had. He never spoke about this, did he? Did you never wonder about what could have happened before he came here? Men can be so incurious sometimes. Is it still a sensitive subject because of the king? Is it important? Please tell me more about Canon Elias' letters to Joseph."

Eustace paused, realising that she was deadly serious. "Please give me a little more time then, to write a transcript to jog my memory."

Only a few days after that he went to find his daughter again. He had seen her go to her bedchamber carrying some clothes. She had had his transcript for two days now and knowing her as he did, she would have read it thoroughly more than once, so he decided this may be a good moment. She never failed to surprise him. There was a large piece of sacking on the bed and on the floor, with some pieces that had been cut from it.

Shaking his head while he made himself comfortable on her clothes chest, he said, "Now please tell me why you are stitching sacking on to your skirt?"

Ceci looked up, almost surprised that he had to ask the question. "Because this is how I must dress from now on. It is only tacked on. And it will protect my clothes. I have sturdy shoes. Lady Elfrida left enough information for me to help the poorest people, including women who are abused or beaten by their husbands, or die in childbirth through ignorance, who live in filthy conditions, who suffer from sores or disease in hovels–places where even the good friars cannot or will not go, or do not understand what can be done. I can make some of her remedies too. Firstly though, I have been to see the bishop".

Eustace's jaw dropped. Ceci pretended not to notice.

"I wanted to ask him if he would request an audience for me with the old Countess of Salisbury, the Lady Ela at Lacock Abbey. You also mentioned that the Master had also been a much sought-after lawyer, as well as the artistic genius we knew him to be. I need enough strength for this, dada, so I feel I need her blessing because I think she will understand. She and her husband were such great benefactors of our cathedral church and knew the Master well. She is very old now and in retirement, no longer the abbess. I shall be most deferential and respectful."

"Did the bishop agree?", was all Eustace could manage.

"Yes," said his daughter. "We are visiting her soon. She may be able to tell me even more about Canon Elias."

"Can we talk about those letters, Ceci? That is why I have come here, you know."

"Yes of course–I have so much on my mind, you see. I have read all you wrote most carefully," she said. "Thank you for remembering all that detail so clearly. I remembered your telling me one day that he was steward to old Archbishop Hubert Walter, who had served King John as well as King Richard–I put two and two together, and thought about such a man in exile in France during the

Interdict. Where else should our new archbishop turn?"

Eustace said: "I think the time Elias spent with Archbishop Hubert was very important. When the archbishop arrived back in this country from the Crusades, he had turned to Elias to help him with a fair national administration system for the Jews living here. Furthermore, Archbishop Hubert had been well known to Jews in the West Country because he had devised a system of equitable weights and measures for their tin miners' stanneries. A uniformity of standard for weights and measures was to be incorporated eventually in Magna Carta.

"Most telling though was that Archbishop Hubert spanned two reigns. When King Richard died, his brother John's claim was dubious, as their elder brother had a son in Brittany. The council chose the man with muscle and power, even though the archbishop had told them it could end in disaster. It is said John murdered that nephew, eventually.

"At his coronation, the archbishop reminded everyone that John was therefore elected in the old Saxon tradition, and he should take the Saxon oath to be a good and just ruler. It was all he could do, he told Elias later; someone who is elected, he supposed, could in theory be unelected, deselected, ejected–and he could only proffer these moral and legal straws to clutch. He knew it wasn't good enough. Kings issued charters and then ignored them. Only the charter issued by the first King Henry had achieved sacred status, kept up at the High Altar in Rochester, by Bishop Gilbert Glanvil.

"Elias learned his lesson well; like Archbishop Hubert, he too was a Glanvil protégé and had read the sacred book of Anglo-Saxon laws kept at Rochester, together with the coronation charter that promised to abide by such custom in principle. Kings always promised much and delivered little. One phrase I remember well was Elias saying that it was all too vague for those dreadful times. He had said that to his mind, laws are only just if all right-minded people agree they are, and when those laws are recorded and enforceable. His words were: "Surely, then, the law is greater than the king. Is that not what the oath should mean?" He knew that the first King Henry's coronation charter would form the best basis for enduring laws, and after Hubert Walter died, he resolved to tell the new archbishop as much.

"The reign was a disaster, as we all know. By 1209, Pope Innocent III had put the country under an Interdict because John had appropriated Church funds for his French wars. The new archbishop, Stephen Langton, whom John refused to accept, was a friend of the pope's and his adviser, a brilliant theologian living and teaching in Paris. From the letters, I could see that Elias wondered what he could possibly know about English politics, or John's deviousness and lack of any morality.

"Elias went to see Archbishop Stephen the next year when he was in exile because of the Interdict, and told him he was going to work for him as a clerk because this new king posed a huge problem that would need the undivided attention of them both. Who but Elias would have dared to do that? He knew they would see eye to eye on many things. But he also said he could only offer advice."

Eustace stood up and stretched his legs. "The barons in England were up in arms because they had to pay a huge tax called 'scutage' to the king if they were not supporting him in the war.

"Let me look at my notes again. I see the archbishop and Elias were back in Canterbury by 1214, but by then the truce that the archbishop was nurturing between the king, pope, and barons was in danger of breaking down, after the king had given away our country to the pope–including an annual payment–in return for his support. Did you know that? That is shocking, isn't it?

"Do you need any more, Ceci? Elias said that they must not put a foot wrong. He still could not believe the king wanted civil war. They must put something within the agreement the barons wanted, while making sure nothing they demanded went against established custom in that coronation charter, but it had to be worded so the king was always kept within the law. And somehow or other it had eventually to be agreed by the pope or it would be ignored. They knew they must not lose sight of this.

"The archbishop doubted their charter's validity in 1215 because of having to coerce the king, and John tore it up as soon as he had sealed it, as we know. But it didn't end there. After John died so unexpectedly the following year, it was reissued twice, modified, and strengthened, but they both knew that until all the parties had accepted it willingly that there would always be doubts. And in the same year as our Trinity Chapel was consecrated, at last the archbishop had achieved that goal. Elias was right about changes, they didn't matter, so long as that all-important principle was kept: that of the king having to obey the law that he himself did not make. They were witnessing the miracle happening."

"Dada, it is fascinating. All these things we didn't know. What I didn't know, of course, was quite how dedicated and how astute our Canon Elias was. You once told me that he saw himself as three people, a priest, an artist, and a lawyer, so it is logical he would see the archbishop in the same way—as a cardinal, as an archbishop and as the country boy he was. All very different."

Ceci was nodding her head. "King John, for all his cunning, must have known he may have met his match in Canterbury. Elias hoped he did not know he was also there. Regardless, any anonymity would have ended at Runnymede because it was Elias who was put in charge of the distribution of the charter. The king had thrown everything behind buying support from the pope. Elias thought the barons' demands were just as unreasonable. No one had any idea that the king was then going to die so quickly.

"Somehow or other they succeeded, didn't they, the archbishop and his so-called 'clerk', even if it didn't look like it at the time. Elias knew—they both knew—that anything less than the king having to obey the law would achieve nothing and serve no purpose. I am so full of admiration for them both. I am not at all surprised that Elias wanted to stay under the parapet. He was exiled when he supported the rebels, I know. But then he came here and gave us our cathedral church. We were so fortunate, weren't we?

"There is a big gap there, though. After King John died, that charter was reissued three times, as I understand it, altered, and maimed as it appeared to be, but without the Master jogging his elbow, the archbishop on his own was negotiating with the pope, and also with the barons about their outrageous demands."

Eustace didn't say so, but he could see that his daughter's

thinking, before he had read those letters, had far outstripped his own: "Yes, it was nowhere near perfect, but it was the beginning of the law being recognised as being above the king. When will you return from Lacock?"

✝

Ceci was only away one night. She arrived back home and sat quietly in the hall, once she had replaced in the oak chest Joseph's neat transcript from Elfrida's sheaf of parchment. Eustace had left the Yard early, anxious about his daughter's visit, so she did not have long to wait.

"You are back," said her father, lamely. He didn't know whether he was worried or perplexed. And he couldn't think why, but he was standing there a little in awe of his daughter. She held out her hands to him.

"Come, sit here. The Lady was very kind to me, and I learned so much that I hadn't known about what had happened before King John died. But that was after she asked me to talk to her about what I wanted to do. She would have liked to have seen the medical notes I spoke of, but I could see her eyes were tired, so I read out one or two passages for her instead.

"We did speak about the Master, too. It was obvious she had known him well. Did you know that the archbishop always called him 'Fenny' because of where he came from? Lady Ela said she had once asked him if he minded, and he had said:

'A Fenny has held the black earth in his hands when it is covered in frost, he has seen the green shoots grow strong in the spring and he has brought in the harvest. He knows too that if only we knew how to drain the land properly, we could feed half of England from there. But that would only be when the roads throughout the kingdom were properly maintained and the poor wretches who attack travellers along their length–because they have no other means of earning a living–are properly supported. And if we ever stop fighting the French, of course.'

"I don't think she could think of an answer to that. The last time she had seen Canon Elias during those years, he was looking strained and ill. He had joined the rebels, as you said, and had spoken out in public against the king and what the pope had done. He was on his way into exile when she had met him again, briefly. He looked bleak. He was carrying one of those old travelling capes they had hidden away for when they needed to escape for a while, just to think and be themselves. He had shrugged; 'Just memories of home,' he said.

"I think it would be best if I wrote about our meeting while it is still clear in my head. But you must hear about the spider's web. When they had been in Canterbury together before the king's treachery at Runnymede, the archbishop had unexpectedly gone into the office that Elias had set up for himself, just off the antechamber. The clerks had been told to try to keep him out of there, the place where the piles of letters and demands and threats of visits ended up.

"Once Elias had sorted through them, he put them into categories: King, Legate, Barons, and assigned them a grade–angry, very angry, and venomous. To spare the archbishop, he and the clerks always syphoned off the first big tranche, which was anything that he thought he could deal with himself.

"Lady Ela then said that Elias had returned, just as the archbishop was staring at the mountain of work: 'Fenny, why didn't you tell me?'

"'Well, Sir,' said Elias–who simply addressed him that way when they were working because, as he said, he was never sure if he was addressing the archbishop, the cardinal, or the country boy from up near Wragby–'there's no point in alarming you unnecessarily.' Quickly and unobtrusively, he had picked up an old sheet of vellum, but the archbishop didn't miss much: 'What is that?'

"'A study in geometry, Sir. It is all perfectly correct. I suppose you might say not so much Euclid, but it could perhaps be one of the six circles of unity, Sir.'

"'If you did it, I'm sure it is whatever you say it is. Let me see.'

"The parchment was duly proffered to the archbishop, complete with its drawing of a perfect spider's web all over it.

"'Fenny, why is your entire right thumb and wrist covering the margin?' The thumb and the wrist were slowly withdrawn to reveal three large black spiders, each hanging by a single thread, one above the other. They all had big teeth and evil smiles. One was wearing a crown; one was wearing armour and carried a sword and the third was the image of the papal legate."

"Lady Ela said there was a long silence at this point.

"'Fenny, why are you holding on so determinedly to the top left-hand corner?' The parchment was reluctantly surrendered. There were two small black flies with worried expressions and bulging eyes, top left.

"The archbishop hardly knew what to say: 'Oh Fenny, is it as bad as this? Let's walk in the woods. Fetch those two old travelling capes, the brown ones that you hid in the muniment cupboard, for when we need to vanish into the trees to escape.

"The Country Boy from up near Wragby and the Fenny went for a walk. It was then that an idea came to the Fenny: 'If we could get hold of some black poplar, if it became tricky, we could smoke the undesirables out of an audience you were giving them. It's evil stuff, especially if it's a bit damp, really useful.'"

Eustace interrupted the flow, laughing:

"When I was a boy, that's what I carried into the Great Hall so many times for the archbishop, when the Master was in exile and then afterwards when he had come to Salisbury."

Then he looked at her and said, "Did Lady Ela give you her blessing, child?"

"Yes, dada! I am so glad I went. Oh, yes. I do feel a lot stronger now. She also told me that she believed that the work I plan to do is essential because so few people try, not having the necessary knowledge."

"Improving such conditions is not really part of the thinking behind the new law. This law is different; it is now much simpler, as the archbishop and his self-styled 'clerk' had hoped, and what is more, accepted by everyone. The charter is also trying to foster trade and markets by encouraging merchants to come here without fear of hindrance, and offering standard weights and measures for goods–all so England can grow strong and prosperous and peaceful. Only then, she believes, will all people be included. I believe she is thinking a long way ahead, but I don't really know.

"She then repeated something Elias had often said: 'What did going to war for gain ever achieve?'

"I asked her what freedom was. She patted my hand and said I was asking the right questions.

"There was only one other subject I touched upon. I asked her what the address the archbishop had given to the people in Salisbury in 1225 had been about. She looked at me and said that I really did understand, didn't I? That same year, in February, Magna Carta had been reissued and at last all had accepted it, and this had been a real triumph for the archbishop who had negotiated it. Then he came here for the consecration of the Trinity Chapel, at Michaelmas, which she thought may have been the first time Canon Elias had seen him in five years, And here was Elias, with his beautiful church, happy at last.

"The archbishop was amazed at the multitude gathered outside. Elias had told him that what he himself was about to do was the culmination of all the dreams they had had while they were in exile, about the reforms they wanted—for the people. Soon there would be vault paintings depicting learning and debating, and a flight of angels praising God would fly from side to side across the cathedral church. At last, as they had wanted, they were starting to bring learning to the people. Their archbishop had delivered Magna Carta to them, setting them on the long path to justice, although they may not yet have understood what that meant. They had all come to hear their great archbishop speak to them.

"She said she was sure she had heard Elias say: 'Just go out there and talk to them about all this, in language they will understand: from the heart. They need to know you are one of them. They will never forget you if you do that.'

"She frowned, as if she wondered if she had heard or remembered that correctly. I smiled to myself and at her. We both knew that she thought she had heard him say such things. By then it was time to leave. She is indeed a remarkable person."

†

The summer passed, and Mabel came to stay for a whole week. We bought some herb plants for my garden, and I kept my head down. She and Bernie needed some time to themselves before he again asks her to marry him, and me to help him build on to the side of his cottage, another little hall with its hearth where they can both live.

Ceci brought back my writings and declared them very useful. She questioned me closely on a remark I had overheard about when Archbishop Stephen had come here for the consecration of the Trinity Chapel in 1225. I didn't know any more than I had written down, other than everybody there had seemed to say the same thing, that his sermon was truly inspired and had seemed to address each person there directly. That young woman has such patience and persistence: "Yes, but can you remember exactly what he said?"

How could I? Thirty-five years had passed, and then I was young and arrogant and stupid. I don't know where it came from, but I blurted out: "He spoke about us, as though he was one of us."

"YES!" she exclaimed. "I think I knew that, after talking with Lady Ela. Don't you see, he was no great nobleman. Like Canon Elias, he was one of us, so he would have seen that charter as being for us, too. That is why what he had said was so inspiring. I haven't mentioned it to my father yet. That reissued charter was newly accepted by all, including the pope, so it wasn't quite as fragile as it once was. Hadn't Canon Elias said to Joseph in one of his letters that this miracle was happening at last?

"The multitude came, hoping their great archbishop would talk to them, so he did. Perhaps he would have told them a little about the struggles over Magna Carta, including his vision for the freedom of the church in England not being controlled by the king. He certainly could have said the charter was endorsed now by everyone and that it set them on the road to justice. He would have explained the new thinking on so many practices, and that the painting up in the vaults in their own cathedral church would reflect learning and debating and all their beliefs, and that the teaching would include them. That address of his to his people, it wasn't in Latin and it wasn't written down, so it must just have come straight from the heart, mustn't it?"

Ceci had learned nothing more from Millie Miller about the well-dressed man. If there was any information to be had, Millie, who was no gossip herself, was always the best person to winkle it out. She did say that she didn't know why else anyone bothered to queue up there, at Fish Stall Number 4. The fish wasn't anything special, but you could learn a great deal about what was going on because Jonah and his cronies were such dreadful old gossips. We had been given an account already of what had happened from Toby, who had been wending his way to the silk merchant's stall for his mother, and had been passing by as voices had been raised. Toby entertained us all with what he had overheard.

"Millie doesn't suffer fools gladly," Ceci says, "but she is so very kind and generous. There would be more hungry people each year if it weren't for her and Sam."

We prayed all summer that the weather would improve, and I don't think it was quite as bad as the previous year, as it turned out. But there was no time for complacency, for in the late Autumn, tragedy overtook Rob's little family.

✝

The urgency of the summons had kept Rob out there into the late evening. There was hardly anyone still around in the market—there never was on a late, cold evening anyway—but Rob's mind was on Sam Miller's roof; Sam should have cut those reeds long before he did. Rob crossed the great square against a sharp wind, and without thinking he kicked discarded carrots and some dung into the water channel at the corner of Endless; better not tell Ellie, women are funny about things like that.

Hastening along the short distance up Endless before taking the turning to his own cottage, he only looked up as he neared his front door. Then he frowned because he could make out the figure of a man bent nearly double, wrapped in a mud-caked cloak. The figure was becoming clearer, leaning hard against a corner, clutching at his side, but holding fast to his satchel. He seemed to then drag his right foot to support himself better in the dirt, so he didn't slip before he spoke. Rob, hurrying now, could only just make out the bloody, bruised face.

"They robbed me and took my horse," the man managed to say.

"Here, let me hold you. Give me your hand. I live just along here, look. Can you put your arm around my neck? Whatever happened? I'll help you in. Ellie will have some broth in the pot. We can lay the cushions near the fire and find some salves. Do you know who did this to you?" He kicked the door hard and shouted to his wife to come quickly.

The man didn't speak immediately, but as he shrank further into the remains of his wrecked clothes he merely pleaded, "May I see Mistress Annie?"

"You are come here to see Annie? I'm afraid she died some three years since. She lived next door to us."

Rob bent down in the gloom and put his hand gently under the man's arm.

"Oh, Wob," the stranger said.

It came like an icy arrow on the breath, and in that same moment it found the unhealed wound. He heard the crunch of the gravel, felt the relief of the drizzle hiding his face. Rob's chest tightened and there was no air. He could see the horse's wet hooves and his own footprints in the grass. He looked around and there was the Master, helping one of the lady's servants position the baggage. Think of that, he told himself, only that, then you may be able to breathe again before you must remember anything more.

The years fell away. He was standing outside Leaden Hall, waiting to lift a small boy onto a great lady's pillion; Mister Gardener and the tiddler.

The Master's sister had allowed the small child she was accompanying to become his constant companion, his helper in the garden for the past two weeks, and his most willing shadow. Almost, he had thought secretly, this little dark-haired boy was the son he may never have, whom he could look after and keep safe.

Very carefully, he picked up the child and swung him behind the lady who smiled and said, "Say thank you to Mister Gardener, Benjamin." The little boy, who no longer had a father of his own, looked down from his lofty seat and put out both his hands, whispering, "Thank you for all of it, Wob."

The big, helpless man would be left only with a memory of those leather laces he was now tucking into the sacking buskins he had made for him. Without the lady ever knowing, since that day until now he suspected they had probably been worn gleefully all night in the bed specially made up for him above the stables.

The lady had turned in her saddle to wrap a travelling cape around him, positioning the folds so the Jew's badge that he must wear did not show. He remembered reaching up and pushing the child's small wooden toy into his lap, before stepping back into the quiet misery he himself had known so often throughout his own childhood, when his own father could not protect him from harm. Who would want to hurt this tiddler, thrown in a river by the fiends who had murdered his parents, the little boy whom he would no longer be able to save? Could this child ever forgive him? The knowledge and the ache of his loss overwhelmed him.

Only a few days before it had been these same good people, together with Mistress Annie Baker, who had wrought a miracle in his own life, all so he could ask Ellie to marry him. Such joy is for sharing and he could not now share his miracle with the tiddler, because he must go away forever, riding on further to some other family, unknown even to him.

The Master had come over to pat the horse with the wet hooves and to gaze long at his sister, until the little group with their servants had moved off and ridden west towards Exeter.

✝

Rob carried the man inside. Ellie scooped up all of Annie Baker's cushions that she had given them and laid them on the floor by the fire. "Here Rob, here", she gestured.

"It's Benjamin. Little Benjamin, do you remember him?" The man was now only half conscious.

"Oh yes, of course I do. I looked after him for the afternoon when all those canons came to listen to Mistress Elfrida's lecture. Pour some water out of that pot and cool it down." She was very carefully removing his coat and opening his shirt under it. Her face turned white:

"Rob, please go to Eustace's house now and send Toby straight home; he'll be talking to Ceci. Then go down to Harnham to find a physician as fast as you can; this is a bad knife wound. I'll fetch some salves. Please hurry. If he comes round properly, I can get him to try a little broth." Rob left, running hard up the street.

Ellie was gently wiping the dirt away when, although the words came in short gasps, he said: "Must get to crossroads. Man from Devizes should wait. Took money, not my shawl, not my treasure." He indicated his satchel. Ellie could see a shawl–his prayer shawl–inside.

"Now," she murmured soothingly, "you rest, I'm going to the outhouse to fetch some salves for you, but first have just a sip or two of my broth." She poured a little in a cup and held it to his lips.

"Only small group of us left in Exeter," he managed to say after drinking the broth, "Could not pay all the tallage this time. King taxes us too much, too much." He closed his eyes against the pain. "We heard: driving us Jews out and attacks in London this year. Some in Tower in London".

As she bathed his hands, he said: "I want to give my treasure to you and Wob."

"No, no. Look, please rest and don't move until I come back from our wash house with the salves. I am lighting this candle from the fire, see, so I shouldn't be long. Toby, our son will be here shortly, and Rob is fetching the physician as quickly as he can."

Holding the candle and shielding it against the wind, Ellie made her way to the outhouse where they washed. It took her a little while feeling along the long shelf, but she found her salves, and made her way straight back. "Here we are," she said.

But there was no one there, just the blood-stained cushions. He had gone, leaving his precious satchel propped up on them.

Ellie looked around in a daze and then rushed to the front door. She could see no one, no one at all. A mist was falling now. She called his name in vain. She knew she must wait for Toby who, on his return, left straight away to search the streets and the market square.

Rob arrived back home to find his wife in great distress, the physician having not yet arrived. He tried to explain that the man had not been at the infirmary when he called, but Ellie was crying quietly by the fire, clutching at the satchel.

"He's gone, but he left us this—his treasure," she said. "Toby is out looking for him."

Rob put his hand on the leather bag. "It's his prayer shawl, isn't it?"

"NO, please don't touch it yet. I haven't looked, but I think I know." She was sobbing now, and she shook as she held onto his arm. Eustace appeared out of nowhere and knelt beside her. "I have just seen Toby," he said. "There is nothing more we can do tonight. I shall be back at daybreak."

No one ever saw Benjamin again. Eustace was so worried he was up before dawn and down in the stables at the Yard saddling up a horse. He rode up Carter Street, warning young Nobby, already in his stables, that he may need him later. He slipped him a coin and rode straight to Rob's cottage. Toby heard him and came outside. They spoke for a moment or two, then Eustace rode on north as far as the crossroads. Nothing, no sign of anyone having been there, so he went on further up the Devizes Road.

Fallen leaves filled the hedgerows and the damp verges betrayed no trampling underfoot. He dismounted from time to time if he thought he had reached somewhere a man could shelter for the night. He called Benjamin's name, and as he heard his own voice, it sounded too loud in the stillness. Nothing stirred in the dark, dank air. Eustace turned back reluctantly when he knew he had long passed the point where an injured man could have come on foot.

Reaching the cottage, he tethered the horse to a nearby post, and went in to find the whole family sitting by the remains of yesterday's fire. Judging by the state of them, no one had been to bed. Rob looked up wearily at his friend: "Sit down with us for a while. Toby has been out again, walking all around here, scouring the streets for any sign. There is no Jewish community here of course and we don't know any of them from Wilton, do we? I keep telling Ellie that if he is alive, he will surely ask someone to find us. He had remembered where Annie's cottage was, hadn't he? Do you think he was worried about bringing his troubles to our house?" Rob bent over as he tried to get up, his joints stiff from the night.

Eustace said: "I must take the horse back to the Yard and then go home to tell Meg. I'll come straight back. Go to bed, both of you, please. Toby, could you stay awake just in case someone comes?"

No one came, not then, not later. Ellie carefully laid Benjamin's prayer shawl on a layer of lavender bags under her clothes in the chest. Rob took the little leather thongs and put them under his side of their mattress.

Each evening when he heard the Compline bell, he held the lion without a tail, with his head bowed as he said a prayer for its lost owner, and then a second one for Annie Baker who had found this toy for him on a market stall, this small wooden lion without a tail, given to the little boy by a man who carved animals for Noah's Ark. Then Rob always prayed for all the people who had ever known and loved Benjamin.

✝

Rob spent too much time mulling over the great harm that had been inflicted upon both him and Ellie when they were children. It ate away at him. He knew he was most fortunate, and he cherished his own son's childhood, wanting to cup it in his hands and keep it forever.

His disgust at all cruelty reached a level he was worried he could not contain. Then this tragedy–the tragedy that nearly broke him–had befallen the family.

"Nothing," he would call out in the night, "must hurt any of us ever again." How could they protect their own dear son?

Toby, my young informant, tells me that only Ellie was truly aware of his state of mind. With a wisdom, gentleness, and will of iron she set about repairing him; to the point where eventually he could accept with equanimity whatever decision his son made about his future, and applaud wherever it was his idealism would take him. Who would have thought she had it in her?

"All it took," said Ellie, simply, "was love."

Part Five

THE QUESTIONS AND THE ANSWERS

Late one afternoon, the two families had gathered in Eustace's hall. Lizzie and Ralph sat together to listen, although both they and Meg were fully aware of why they were there and already suspected what they would hear. They had just returned from delivering bread and a large bowl of potage to the friars to distribute, a twice-weekly necessity these chill days.

Toby knelt and put his arms around his mother and pressed her head into his chest. He stroked her hair, but was looking up at his father as he spoke.

"The world outside is creeping in here and we cannot stop it. Someone attacked Benjamin, maybe just because he was a Jew. The king prepares for war, so communities are taxed beyond endurance. For all we know the king is always preparing for war.

"Lady Ela told Ceci she has heard that absentee post-holders are being appointed by the king to positions in cathedral churches they have no intention of ever visiting, despite the clause in that charter declaring that the English Church shall remain free from interference in its elections. Of course, the pope supports the king now—and against us, if that is what the king wants.

"Sir Gilbert's man revealed to me their hopes that, in our country, the law and not the king will always be supreme—to prevent injustice, because the king should obey that law too. And it will be other people who make that law, not the king alone.

"Ceci and I have never seen that Great Charter, but each time it is reissued, whatever else is updated, that principle must remain. So, as Ceci understands it from the Master's letters, over the years it almost won't matter so much which other clauses are written in, or are taken out as no longer relevant."

Ceci stepped away from the post she had been resting against. "Toby is right," she said, smiling fondly at him. "You all know now that I have been to speak with Lady Ela at Lacock Abbey, who shared her wisdom with me. She and the Earl were great benefactors of our cathedral church. And it was that Great Charter itself that she called upon to save her from being made to marry again when everyone else assumed–wrongly–that her husband must be dead. I understand we have our own engrossment of the earliest one from 1215, in Salisbury. I believe it is our treasure.

"Now, we don't know that Benjamin never reached the crossroads, do we? He may have done, or perhaps the man he was meeting came further down the road to Salisbury looking for him? Or perhaps Rob was right when he said Benjamin may not have wished to bring his troubles here, only his treasure.

"Each night, when he hears the Compline bell, Rob prays for him; it is all we can do. But you see, Benjamin believed he had left his treasure in a safe place, whatever would befall him.

"That is exactly what Lady Elfrida did when she entrusted her precious work to you dada, when she put it in the oak chest. She knew she was dying. You just assumed it was part of her testimony, and Joseph transcribed it because he is so diligent, but he didn't use it because it was not relevant to what he was doing.

"I found the transcription one day, slipped in with Joseph's other work. She had judged well. Solomon the apothecary she worked with in Norwich would not need it, but here she gave us all she had learned in a lifetime.

"This is now my special task. I see you all looking at the depth of old sacking I have tacked up around my hem and the half-sleeves from my elbow. The places I must go mean I should be dressed like this; I have veils to keep out foul air. I have Mistress Elfrida's work from her time in this country as well as in Spain, where she learned so much more from the Moors and from the Jews who were there. I can surely bring some comfort and relief.

"We know from the Scriptures we are charged with caring for

the old and the sick and the very poor. Here in Salisbury, we have always fed and clothed them in times of hunger and repaired their shelters. And as well as this work, in addition to running the forge and the shop, surely Lizzie and Ralph soon will have babies to look after too, because they are our future.

"I cannot stop thinking about that charter, that new written law we don't think any other country has in this way. Is this the right way? It is good that clauses are changed because then it is re-issued, Lady Ela said. King John had refused to accept the appointment of a new abbot for Saint Edmundsbury in 1215–the same year as our original charter–on the grounds that the abbey's old charter was no longer valid because it had not been used for so long.

"Archbishop Stephen and the Master took a huge risk with the barons in the drafting, with the principle of the supremacy of the law tucked in it, to be there always as a curb on the king, who had after all paid money to the pope to support him. That is not a pretty picture, is it? In this world now, as far as I know, nowhere else has a written law like that, it is almost unthinkable.

"The pope and his archbishop; those two brilliant minds, those friends in Paris all those decades ago who had imagined they could save the world between them, with their integrity, their scholarship and meticulous examining of the scriptures. How betrayed must our cardinal archbishop have felt at that moment? And the pope when his cardinal, his adviser, had to go in a different direction as archbishop to a forsworn king? Then this pope, who had been his great friend, died. What a tragedy it all was.

"After the king had repudiated the charter he had sealed, it was Canon Elias and Simon Langton, the archbishop's brother, who bore the brunt in agreeing to risk joining the rebels and the French prince when he came here to try to depose the king. They stood up in public, in London at St Paul's Cross, and denounced what the king had done and said he had misled the pope and so the excommunications the new pope had announced were therefore not valid. The archbishop did not want to leave England because the English Church was too important for him to abandon his duty here, but he had already defied the pope in not excommunicating the rebels when he was ordered to do so. And so he did have to go back into exile when it all broke down after Runnymede.

"But you see how, come what may, they supported each other, always. Possibly, they knew the path they set this country upon was in real danger of being swept over the precipice by opening the floodgates to more civil war. We'll never know what strain they were under.

"It was old William Marshall, the Earl of Pembroke, acting as Regent because he was Rector of the Council, who saved the charter when he amended and reissued it the next year, within a month of King John's death. That was probably the wisest decision he ever took in his life, although he didn't know it. He too had started off in life as a nobody, a younger son having no lands to inherit. It does not matter at all that the charter has been improved upon and updated twice since then.

"It is no small wonder is it that Canon Elias rose no further in the Church, and in fact never wanted to. 'Safer under the parapet,' was how Lady Ela expressed it. And furthermore, he never talked about it here. In that way he and Archbishop Stephen kept faith with one another until the day the archbishop died. My father said that in one of Annie's testimonies she had said that for all the tragedies that befell them here, the only time she ever thought the Master may have been crying was when he came into the kitchen to tell her of Archbishop Stephen's death. The archbishop left him his treasured breviary in his will, Lady Ela said.

"He was our Canon Elias, this nobody, this genius, this visionary, this man of God." She brought her fist down hard on their board, at which she was standing. She didn't mind that it hurt because some things need emphasising. Ceci took her mother's hand. Toby got up off his knees and stood by his father.

He said, "No pressure has been put on me to join de Montfort. Tentatively, I have only been offered a position as a courier into Gloucestershire. We don't know what is coming, do we? And I know I must look after my parents. So, what should I do?" He looked at everyone gathered there. "These are the things I know:

"This man, de Montfort, believes that somehow our

country's future lies here, and that he and others after him may have to fight for this charter to remain part of our law. I don't know how, but that seems to be a principle for which the Master was prepared to sacrifice everything, even his chance of making a reality of our glorious cathedral church.

"My father knows what having no protection from injustice and brutality means. Could a law prevent that?

"But I have found that there are many strands to this thread; my mother is naturally an expert on such things. One Tuesday Market she asked me to fetch an order for silk thread she had placed with a merchant who trades here. I did so, but as he looked as if he was a well-travelled man, I took the chance to ask if he had heard of Simon de Montfort. He had, of course. He spoke of the 'Provisions of Oxford' two years ago and of de Montfort's wish to have more people like us involved in government, all because of Magna Carta, as it is called in Latin. But then he said that de Montfort was also well known for persecuting the Jews. Naturally, this horrified me, so I moved on and asked a wool trader who also has connections to the outside world, and he had heard much the same story.

"So, what am I to do now? I cannot help to persecute anyone. I do not believe that is right, so I only believe in half of his message. Once, the Master had to make his choice; he knew how important it was above all things to bring the king inside the law. He kept that cathedral church inside his head completely in the background, even though hitherto it had been his greatest wish.

"Ceci has given me her counsel. She also knows she can, and must do what she believes to be right. Ceci now has the knowledge she needs. It was Lady Elfrida's gift to us. I can't help calling her Lady Elfrida. I know she wasn't, she was a nobody, like us, but to all who met her here, I understand she was a very great lady indeed. Ceci cannot make use of all her work as she is not trained, and she suspects that no one here is, but it is a beginning, and she will do all she can.

"Of course, we are different, Ceci and I, but it doesn't matter because having such choices is how we would both wish to live in a new age. We know we are nobody in this world where, as yet, only the strong and the powerful rule, but then we know the great archbishop, that country boy from up near Wragby, and Canon Elias the Fenny, as Lady Ela said they had sometimes described each other, also started out as nobodies too, didn't they? Without their faith and their determination and bravery, we would not be sitting here discussing this.

"If this is not the age that is coming and we are both wrong, and this is not even the way in which such an age will dawn, then we pray that one day that age will come, and that meanwhile you will be able to forgive us for setting out on whichever road we both take, and our reasons for taking it.

"Our parents have agreed to talk to the gentleman who comes into the ironmonger's, then we shall all have heard his story, but the choice is for us, for Ceci and me, to make. We hoped this man could come to Salisbury this evening, but he said he may have another engagement.

"I know now that I shall have to say no to his offer. I understand that Eustace wishes to write to Joseph, of course I do. I expect this man will continue to collect his packages.

"What Eustace does is for him to decide, it is his choice to make, you see.

"How can de Montfort's cause be my cause? When you cease to be a simple man who always does what he is told, when you become free in your head in fact, the world becomes complicated. I can make a choice, but it cannot be a hot-headed choice, can it?

"It is idealism itself that is a thread woven from many strands. However much I support his efforts to include us ordinary people in government, I cannot support the persecution of any peoples, and not just because they happen to be ones my father has known. I have made my choice.

"I hardly dare think any further about where these ideas about freedom and choice and the future could take me, because suppose I was told to do something in which I do not believe, what then would my choice be?

"A while ago now, I had a vivid dream about a bell. It was here; a beautiful, glorious bell, still in the foundry. I searched for it in the Chequers, but I could find neither it, nor the foundry. Perhaps that bell is for the future then? Perhaps a time will come when I, or someone like me, could assist this cause. I have weighed it in the balance, and that time for me is not now. I shall not be helping this man and riding off with him, and that is not because I don't think that the charter is right, because I do.

"And were I in a parliament such as de Montfort envisages, I would have to be brave and say what I think without fear, would I not? I see now how difficult it all can be. Perhaps I am growing up.

"I am the son of a free man, not tied to the land as so very many are. I could, in my dream had I wished, been taken on as an apprentice at the bell foundry, or as happened, just smiled and walked away, imagining the tones and notes. I heard the choice as music in my head. Perhaps this bell was not for me, but even in my dream I had a choice, you see. How many people like my father have any kind of choice? My father had been unfree, a serf. Perhaps this charter that wants justice for free men could herald the end of being unfree, and that making such choices is the future for all of us? We don't know, but I do know that making a choice is not always an easy thing to do. He glanced at Lizzie and smiled wryly. It is time for me to learn Latin, I think. We do have a justice system in this country, but how little any one of us here knows about it. Our instinct is to keep well away from a court of law. How could we go to Westminster, even if only for Common Pleas? I believe I need to understand much more, just as Ceci learns more everyday about Lady Elfrida's remedies.

"We both know that we must keep faith and believe that what we do to help the poor and the less able, and the weak and the sick will make a difference. There is nothing else, is there? We cannot prevent our landscape or the people in it from changing, so we think it would be better if we went out there, to become a part of it."

✝

So far, neither Eustace nor Meg nor Lizzie nor Ralph had spoken. Nor had Rob or Ellie. Eustace was right in assuming they would all be of one mind:

Yes, they think. You do have choices, as do we all. You must both do what you believe to be right. In your hearts stay here with us too, for out there are the terrors of the night, and we cannot face them without you.

It was late when everyone had agreed there was nothing left to say. Ellie stood between her husband and her son, with her head held high.

The bell for Compline rang out as they left Eustace's hall, his family standing with them outside on the path. Rob had brought the lion without a tail with him, tucked in the inside pocket of his jerkin. At that moment they were all looking up beyond the infinite stars, to where they knew the angels would be keeping watch.

As they stood with their thoughts, a man on horseback rode up. He dismounted, bowed to each of the four women and said: "I must apologise for being so late, I was detained in Gloucester. If they are at home, I would stay with relatives nearby and I could come back tomorrow if you wish, and if it is convenient?" Eustace was about to speak, when he realised the man was leaning against his horse and gazing at Ellie. "Pray, forgive me, Ma'am," he said, "I know it is only by the light from that lovely fire in there, but it is quite uncanny; you are the image of the wife of one of my elder brothers."

As the little group was caught between not showing shock and preventing the silence becoming too long, it was quick-thinking Meg who said, "Thank you, Sir", as she dropped him a small curtsey. "I am Mistress Clerk, wife to Eustace here who is assistant clerk of the works at our cathedral church, and the mother of Cecily, whose acquaintance I believe you have already made? Would it perhaps be more convenient for you to call next Wednesday? I believe that is the day you come to the ironmonger's shop. My husband, Eustace, can be at home if you wish."

The man smiled at them all and touched his hat. "Yes, indeed, thank you so much. That is very thoughtful of you." He took his leave at once, mounted his horse and rode up the street in the direction of the river.

They all looked at one another. Ceci took Ellie by the arm and gently led her back inside to a seat by the fire. "Come and sit here," she said, "just until you have some colour back in your cheeks."

Meg said, "I have gained us five days, that is all. This is still a problem for both our families, especially for poor Ellie who may have more shocks to come, we don't know. Toby has already given us his opinion and we shall respect that."

Lizzie had noticed something that the others had missed. "He wasn't wearing his smart red leather shoes, nor his embroidered gloves that everyone talks about. I wonder where he leaves them? It isn't with his relatives, because he seemed unsure they were even there. Someone else must be helping him."

Ralph, who had not spoken at all that evening, interrupted, "I am about to join this family, so I hope I may speak. Ever since I began my apprenticeship here, I have watched and marvelled at how close you all are, and how you support and help each other–so much so I find it quite difficult to think of you as two families at all. In my head Ellie will become my kin too. I hope that is alright?"

Rob exclaimed, "It'll be like having another son, lad." Toby clapped him on the shoulder and Ellie looked up at him gratefully. Ralph went to kneel beside her and said, "As Lizzie just remarked, there may well be someone else here who is helping him, and I have a feeling I have seen this man somewhere before but I am not sure. Will you let me think about it?"

The next day he told Lizzie that he had remembered where that was. The man, who was dressed very differently then, had hired a horse and some panniers from young Nobby the carter, whilst he had been at the stables talking to his friend Barnaby. The man had just said he had 'big things to move' with no further explanation. "I'm not sure I like things I don't know about," said Ralph. Only a little remark, but it all added to a sense of unease.

Lizzie and her mother had previously been quietly discussing the problem, Lizzie replied to Ralph, "Mother and I were both wondering how safe it may be to use their courier. What would happen if the king's men intercepted one of these letters or psalteries? We cannot leave Joseph in ignorance though, can we? However, I think we have agreed on a way to solve the problem."

Upon hearing Ralph's news, Eustace decided that he would have a quiet word with Nobby, who was the one person he knew who was least likely to listen to gossip. "We don't even know his name. Perhaps everyone noticed his shoes just because they were unsuitable for negotiating the mud and the mess in our marketplace. Who was he trying to impress? Nobby is a sound man, and he should at least be told the little we have learned."

✝

They are so good, my new-found friends. They have asked all four of us to Eustace's hall for Christmas Day. I have never been invited out on Christmas Day before, and I don't think Bernie has been, either. Bernie did say were they really sure about Nobbut being there with their cat, but Mistress Meg assured me it would be alright. We shall have to make sure Nobbut is well groomed though, remembering her reaction to the livestock in that soldier's beard!

Sometimes, I suppose we are still trying to understand one another. Eustace has asked me one or two strange questions lately, such as has Bernie ever ridden further than Wilton? How does he think we earn our living if we don't go to inspect all the oak we buy? Bernie and I agree that the best oak from around here comes from near Chippenham, but one or other of us will always ride up there to choose it, and to anywhere else with a good reputation, if there is some wood to be cut. We take two of the carpenters with us for protection on the roads, as well as teaching them what they should be looking out for.

I shall take these latest pieces of writing with me at Christmas and write up anything more they may have, as I said I would finish by the end of this year. I always ask them to run their eyes over it to see if I have been accurate enough in recording what they told me.

I have made two lightweight wooden crutches for Ned. Ellie fashioned good padded pieces for the top parts around his elbows that I was able to splice in. I found strong sticks with a curved part set at an angle and when I measured them against his arms; they were just right, so I also spliced in another piece for a handle. He has always resisted anything like this until now. He practised for days, using them with his good leg, and now he manages very well at home and in the garden, and he went by himself with them as far as Bernie's yesterday. This is wonderful progress. We take them with us in his new barrow-cart and Nobbut sits on the other side. Ned put his head back this morning, as I was pushing it and looking up at me, with the sun shining on his face, he said he now has everything he wants in the world.

We are all looking forward to Christmas, when Ceci says she hopes we'll all go into church together before we go back to Eustace's hall. Ned understands so much more these days. He loves his new barrow-cart, and he thinks his Mistress Cecily is wonderfully kind. What a year this has been; I can't imagine anything as good as all this will ever happen again. Before we return home in the evening, we'll listen for the Compline bell together and go outside to look up beyond the stars, for our guardian angels. Rob will have his treasure with him, I am sure.

I still listen for the bell every evening; it marks my bedtime, when I thank the angel who is looking after my Ned, although of course God knows so much more about angels than I do. Well, He would, wouldn't He?

†

The gentleman with the red leather shoes came into the ironmonger's shop to collect his package. Toby was talking to Ceci behind the counter. She was dressed for the visits she had to make that morning. They had just agreed between them that he should act as escort on the 'little errand' they had planned, after Christmas once the weather had improved.

They had discussed at length how best to break the news to the gentleman that neither Ceci nor Toby would be able to assist him, having initially agreed to stick to the original plan to allow him to visit Eustace at home as arranged, because there was no privacy in the shop. Nonetheless, unable to resist their curiosity, Rob and Ellie were hovering out of sight with Eustace and Meg in the room behind. "This is silly," hissed Meg. "Shush!" whispered Ellie. "Why didn't he give us his name?" They all shook their heads.

They heard him say to Ceci, "Dear young lady, I have come to apologise profusely. Unknown to me until yesterday evening, someone from Chippenham has joined us who can both read and write, and he has also offered to ride the short distance into Gloucestershire each week, so the man I serve will arrange for future deliveries to be made instead to the Chippenham wheelwright. I am so sorry; I don't know what to say except to thank you all for your kindness in considering my original request."

He half turned and opened the palms of his hands; "Of course the lady who looks so like my sister-in-law is not here. I don't know how well you know her family? Margaret is older I think, but the image of her father. He was one of those knights who owed service to the king for lands in Normandy, where he was sadly killed in that disastrous campaign, when Margaret was but a child.

"She had already joined her wider family I'm sure, because her mother had died of a fever before Margaret was two. It's a big family. I have been racking my brains trying to remember any other brothers and sisters who looked like William. Anyway, I'm sure the lady would know somewhere along the line if they are her kin too. I stayed with Margaret and my brother the night I came over last week, but they couldn't think of anyone, so perhaps I am mistaken.

"I wish you a good day and thank you again for your time and your consideration, and to you too, of course, Sir. Perhaps you could explain it to Mister Eustace for me?" He removed his hat and bowed to Toby as he left. Toby followed him out, shook hands with him outside, came back inside and closed the door. He leaned against it while he collected himself, then said, "We never did find out who that gentleman was, did we? And it doesn't matter, does it?"

As he looked up, they all came out of the backroom and into the shop. Ellie said, "I know who I am. I am Rob Gardener's wife and the mother of Toby Gardener." Toby said, "Yes, you are, but you are also Ellie Gardener, and we all love you."

Ceci smiled at her, "I don't think it matters at all who your father was. There will never be a truer knight, or as perfect and gentle as my Toby, will there?"

No one said anything. In fact, they may all have been holding their breath. Toby gazed at her for more than eight, nine, ten heartbeats. He hadn't noticed that particular freckle on the tilt of her nose until now.

After thoughts

My name is Lizzie Clerk. You will have heard of me by now. Today, on Christmas morning, as we were waiting for everyone to arrive before heading to the cathedral church together, my father reminded me that I hadn't yet given my story to Mister Woodman, as he continues to call himself. Well, I wanted to write this myself. He knows we know who he is, but there is still a lot he doesn't know, which is one reason why today will be such fun. I think Nobbut can only sit by the long bench for the infirm in the cathedral church, so I'm sure all of us will stand there too.

I didn't really want to write anything much, because when I read all the other contributions, my life didn't seem to be as interesting as everyone else's. Ellie and Rob must have been so strong to have come through all they had to endure, and fancy my own dada being that well-travelled, and working for bishops.

We children know each other well of course because we were brought up together. From what they say, I suspect I was always seen as the ringleader. I don't think I always was really, but I am like my mother–having some enterprise and a little naughty streak, I suppose. It makes life bright, doesn't it? Toby was so nice, and so decent that as a child he was always very easy to lead astray. I shall never forget that kipper-box helmet.

Now he is someone else. He is thoughtful and he has principles. Charming yes, but much more than that. He would do well in one of those parliaments or whatever it is they keep talking about, if they ever happen. I can't imagine it, but one day in the future, perhaps someone like him? Who knows? The world would have to change a lot first, and we all have a long way to travel for that to happen, some further than others and that includes the miserable people who own Fish Stall Number 4.

Toby has become a thinker, rather than a dreamer. This brings me to Ceci, of course. I suspect I shall never tell her quite how much I admire her. She will have to read it here. If women were ever allowed to do anything much that is useful in this world, it would all be easier for her. She needs a strong, good man. I was never sure if either of them could see they were made for each other. But now–At last! At last!

My father suggested I call this short piece a 'postscript'. I could see what he was up to and said no very firmly to his Latin. I told him that these are my "After thoughts".

"Stubborn to the end, " he told Ralph. "But I would have liked to have seen her stand up to my mother, when she was in the kitchen at her Friday scrubbing-bench. She came from over the border (he never said which border) and was very short-sighted. She would always peer to see whether it was a girl or a boy she had sitting in turn on it. Girls she would treat to 'slummocky little mawther', as she tried to remove every last freckle with her scrubbing brush." So, that was what dada would mutter under his breath if I was late for something or other, untidy and racing to the door, clutching some last garment to put on or tie up or whatever it was.

My parents have been wonderful. Ceci and I had such a happy childhood. I can only say sorry for my nature. I know my mother and I are alike in a lot of ways. We stand in the kitchen and eke out our flour, as well as all the extra Millie gives us in these hard times, so we can make as much bread as possible every day. We live each day as it comes. Sometimes we flick flour at each other if one of us makes the other laugh, or I will throw a bean up in the air for her to catch. She calls me the Bean Queen because I soak the dried peas and beans overnight and stew them with herbs, so they taste nice. Why shouldn't poor people have food that tastes nice too? There are so many hungry people we take food to this time of year. Ellie comes down here at least twice a week with the clothes she has mended and refurbished for them. Sometimes she sews ribbons on the bodices as well. She thinks like we do. Such a sweetheart! But all this isn't very exciting, is it?

Soon Ralph and I will marry. We have waited such a long time to be married, but he had to finish his apprenticeship before he was even allowed to ask me, formally. He has no close family of his own, and I think he was rather shy. I knew from the first day I set eyes on him, but I have learned to be patient. Well, almost.

I can also do household accounts quite accurately now. I still like Big Meat and he won't be getting liver or tripe. I had better confess there were even more noughts on those silver pennies for meat before Toby told me to take them away. He asked me if big meat really cost that much and I said I didn't know, but I didn't want to end up with liver or tripe, so he said subtract one nought from each and I should still be alright. He was wise, even then. Ralph and I are going to live at the ironmonger's shop as soon as we are married and we have made our rooms there look just how I want them to look.

What a dear Toby is. I kept telling Ceci she would have to nudge him eventually. His speech the other evening affected us all. I am just so pleased for them.

Reggie, with Ned and Nobbut and Bernie, all turned up here this morning, looking extremely smart. Bernie thoughtfully brought his own heavy-duty stool to sit on at our board, and he and Ned had groomed Nobbut thoroughly and arranged those curls on the top of his head so beautifully he could have been leading a procession from the Bishop's Palace. Well, perhaps not, but that is the poshest place I can think of in Salisbury. On S. Thomas' day in a few days' time, we shall all go into the market square as well to watch their procession.

My father had rolled up the letter he had written and sealed and addressed it. He left it on top of the oak chest and said to Reggie he would be grateful if he and Bernie would deliver that letter there on the oak chest for him, sometime in the new year. Reggie said, "Yes, of course." We were all waiting for him to pick it up and read the address, but it seemed to be forever and a day before he walked over there.

So much emotion. They are fine people. We love Nobbut of course (who wouldn't?) and Ceci has a special, caring friendship with Ned.

I know this world can be frightening and horrible. I'm not silly, even if dada says, "That girl doesn't talk, she chatters." I used to stand in S. Thomas' Church and wonder why God couldn't make it all better, but it is all of us who are supposed to listen and act, and be kind to each other and not be greedy because we make the world what it is, don't we?

And if people don't behave well, how do you make them? With good laws that include everyone I suppose. I know I am not as clever as some of the other people here, but I do try.

All will be well. We hope all will be very well for our new friends. We have decided between us that we shall look after them, whatever life throws at us, whenever they may need us, so that's a start on the road, isn't it?

I must stop being such a chatterbox. I thought I said I wasn't going to write very much…

✝

Those were Lizzie's After thoughts, and here are mine. As the member of the family I know least about, she is quite a surprise isn't she? I can't help smiling at her and liking her. Seeing how well Eustace and Meg do together, she and young Ralph should have a similarly interesting marriage!

Christmas was the most unforgettable of days. We went to the cathedral church, all twelve of us, altogether. I don't know why being together was so important, but it was.

Ned seemed to follow everything, and he kept smiling at me. He loves to sing, so we sang carols, and then more carols in Eustace's hall. They must have been out the day before, cutting evergreens and holly in abundance. The yule log was brought in, but it had to wait until we had cleared the board. Two geese and some boar brawn and so many vegetable, fruit and meat Christmas pies arrived, (such a relief you only have to eat the fillings) and then custards and jellies. Ned couldn't stop smiling.

The ale was mercifully weak because Eustace said he had something special as Meg came in, carefully carrying a large jug of mulled wine. Once dinner was done the board was cleared and stored away because there were so many of us. Then the Yule log could be dragged to the hearth amidst much cheering and laughter. I don't know why we were all laughing, perhaps it was the wine.

Eustace had put a sealed parchment scroll on his oak chest and asked me if Bernie and I would deliver it sometime in the new year. I said yes of course we would, but I only went over to look at the name and destination when Nobbut decided to investigate.

I cannot tell you how much I was shaking. Bernie came over and I whispered the address to him. We stood and stared together. Oh Bernie. Oh Reggie. How?

They had thought it all through, of course. Ceci and Lizzie and Ralph would look after Ned and Nobbut between them. Ned could have a special corner to sit in the ironmonger's shop, in charge of twine and string and counting out the fiddly things. His face was a picture of utter delight when they told him, he really did understand everything these days. Rob would tend my garden. Toby was coming with us to make sure we behaved ourselves and didn't get lost. Jonathan had agreed already that he could run the business for us, meanwhile. Sworn to secrecy, he had never said a word to us!

The canon chancellor had given Eustace details of the route they had taken two years prior and had given us accommodation on the way there and on the way back, while we were still in the Salisbury diocese. No letter had ever been sent in either direction between the abbey or the cathedral church to say that either Joseph or Eustace were ill (such a possibility had been mooted before they departed two years ago.) Eustace knows the canon chancellor quite well these days as they have been in discussion about the idea of schools teaching children the importance of this new law, and even about Magna Carta's origins.

Joyous, just joyous. That night, when we arrived home, as I left Bernie at his door, he said: "Is there a river in Saint Edmundsbury? May I bring my hat?" We started laughing again and we couldn't stop. Ned was asleep in his barrow-cart with Nobbut anxiously protecting him, probably from the two silly old men, laughing helplessly and holding onto the alder trees outside Bernie's cottage.

✝

Magna Carta is for when we dare to think about our future, but our future is something we cannot know. The great archbishop and our own

Canon Elias had such vision, but there are no easy answers for us now.

Those answers don't always involve the law; it is just the way our society works that is difficult. All Ceci is planning to do is so very valuable, but it is shameful, isn't it, that it has to happen at all. Toby, daring to think about the implications of freedom, and each year Meg and Lizzie and Ellie and Rob are all feeding and clothing and repairing the hovels of the poor and the unfree. Something is wrong. Is it like this because other people are too uncaring, too rich and too powerful?

What that soldier did to Ned was terrible, a crime that went unpunished. Even if he did not mean to do it, not acknowledging it was the act of a coward. I had no recourse to the law, but it didn't stop Ned being given all the love and care he was due.

What happened to Vivie and Maudie brought me to my knees. Until our society changes, as far as I know, that would not be punishable by the law, would it? It drove both of them mad, and I still feel so helpless. All Bernie and I can do is to support the good friars.

And Rob and Benjamin: Benjamin's assailant wounded him with a knife, he may even have killed him. That was a crime, and he should be punished, but what could Magna Carta on its own have done about the way we treat foreigners? Surely understanding and compassion comes from somewhere else first?

It is 1260, but I can't see many signs that King Henry is ruling much better than his father did, even if he is not cruel and corrupt. The barons are in revolt again, and he still goes to war. He interferes in church elections, so they say. But the idea, the perception that we keep to the old customs is there, for this is the body of our common law. We do not ever forget that. The king agreed that a council or parliament would vote him money from taxes, and he cannot go against that. Surely this is what is being bedded down.

One day, perhaps we shall all be free, but we have no way of knowing. This Simon de Montfort, whoever he is, is certainly right in some regards: knights of the shire and burgesses having a say in what goes on in government sounds like a good idea to me. But of course, everyone, including the king, must see it that way.

Yes, Toby and Ceci have learned a great deal. They dare to ask the big questions and are not afraid of saying they don't have the answers.

I'm sure Canon Elias knew all this; he never seemed to be afraid.

Justice is about much more than laws. We all must change; surely our whole society has to change. Can it? No king, no pope wants his authority challenged. Then the truth hit me: our great charter does indeed challenge the king's authority unless he recognises that here, the law is absolute. Ceci is right, of course. In Salisbury we have our own engrossment of the very first Magna Carta and it is our treasure, but ideas in it will surely lead to trouble in some future time.

I came near to despair that evening, until I heard Jeffrey say: "That's how things are. Now get working on it."

"Yes, Jeffrey," I said.

In the contributions I have received from Eustace and Ceci, they have confirmed what I had already known deep down, that it was indeed Canon Elias who had given away his travelling cape to Vivie. And come to think of it, when Bernie and I had first gone to see him, the elderly friar had never contradicted me when I had told him what I supposed about the travelling cape. They were also sworn to secrecy, so I shall never know whether they also understood how important it was to her. Does it matter?

The new law exists, and that does matter; we believe it is a true beginning. At this moment it may be a small flame, illuminating for those who govern us much that is wrong. In a future time surely, everyone should have a right to justice under the law, including Vivie, and those who are yet un-free. We must do all we can to grow with it, but justice and life itself are much more than laws. Eustace cannot come with us to see Joseph, because he will be working on the new chapter house and cloisters, but his generosity and selflessness are an inspiration, and that is also what life is all about, isn't it?

Joseph, Joseph! So much lost time to make up. I don't know why my life has been so blessed, when I have been so foolish. I think yours has been blessed too, my wise little brother? In our own way, we are all striving for a better world, aren't we?

✝

Sue Allenby is a Cathedral guide and lives in Salisbury. She studied medieval history and architecture and wrote her first novel *Elias: A Story of the Founding of Salisbury* for the Cathedral's 800th anniversary in 2020.

Magna Carta ~ Conversations in Salisbury 1260 is her second novel set in this 13th century city. She says she grew so fond of some of her characters in Elias, it was hard to let them go.

Printed in Great Britain
by Amazon